HEMINGWAY'S
SUITCASE

HEMINGWAY'S
SUITCASE

LELAND C. SHANLE JR.

Manufactured in the United States

Paperback Edition ISBN: 978-0-9837107-3-8
eBook Edition ISBN: 978-0-9837107-4-5

Cover Art: Bogdan Maksimovic
Cover and Interior Design: Creative Publishing Book Design

To Laura Lynn

THE BATTLER

8 July 1918

A Red Cross Ford Model T ambulance struggled through the rutted mud, its twenty-horsepower engine varying its pitch like a whining child as the wooden-spoked wheels alternately spun and gained traction through thin rubber tires. Behind the steering wheel an eighteen-year-old bright-eyed lieutenant fought the rough road, and in the back, boxes of cigarettes and chocolates—the ambulance's only contents—bounced around. Bombs and mortars burst around the vehicle, but the driver was cloaked by the invisible shield of youth, and made his way forward fearlessly.

A putrid brown snake wound through the hills and mountains outside of Fossatta di Piare on the Italian front. Trenches on the other side of the no-man's-land, the Austro-Hungarian side, sent the artillery and mortars that shrieked through the sky and tore at both mud and man.

As he bounced to a stop on the lip of a trench, the lieutenant shut off the engine and looked up at the crystal-clear Italian sky. Its sun beat down on the trenches. He hoped it would dry the mud and flatten the ruts. Reaching outside the window, he squeezed a rubber bladder that blew air through a brass horn, announcing his arrival.

Mud-caked creatures emerged from all along the trench, drawn by the sound of the horn, each topped with a steel helmet. Austro-Hungarian interest had moved down the firing line, giving the mud creatures momentary safety. White eyes shone over white teeth as the creatures became men.

The lieutenant got out of the ambulance and handed out tokens of civilization. Matches struck off the dashboard, the only clean surface within miles, and lit cigarettes. Blue smoke wafted between the mud men as they ate chocolate. Indiscernible by age or feature, they delighted in the luxury of the soft chocolate and harsh smoke. It was a moment of tranquility. But a temporary one. A mortar exploded among them. The world spun in a tsunami of destruction. Confusion reigned.

Rolling in the mud and blood, the lieutenant groped for clarity. He fought the chaos that ruled his brain. Men's mouths let out screams he could not hear. Blood oozed from wounds he could not feel. Mortars continued to fall. Struggling to get upright on his shredded legs, one thought formed: he must get the wounded to an aid station.

A concussion raged through his head as he gathered the survivors under direct fire. Crimson blood stained the mud men who writhed on the ground. Those who could, scrambled back to the trench.

Those who couldn't, were loaded onto the ambulance. Those that didn't writhe at all, were left. They would return to the mud, as one.

The lieutenant choked the throttle, flipped on the ignition, then stumbled to the front of the vehicle, inserted the crank wrench, and furiously spun the engine. It caught, idling quietly as mortars crashed down with a deafening roar.

Overloaded, the ambulance fought mud, mortars, and weight as it struggled toward the battlefield aid station. Moans filled the lieutenant's ears; he was shocked to realize some were his own. His vision began to close in from the edges—the consequence of blood loss. It seemed to flow directly from his eyes onto the floor board. Immortality and the shield of youth were gone—forever.

As he slid to a stop at the aid station, the ambulance's left front wheel splintered when he turned the steering wheel hard to the right. The vehicle jolted to a stop as the axle dug in, and he was flung from the cab.

Lying in the soft warm mud, he let consciousness slip away, feeling certain that death would follow.

Time became an abstract concept—something lost and unable to be deciphered. Meaningless units passed... or didn't. He floated among them.

A sharp sound violated his purgatory; bright light blinded him. Was this it? Judgment day? Redemption? Would Peter give him a thumbs up or down?

"Time to wake up, Lieutenant."

An angel's voice? Or a demon's? Heaven or Hell?

He opened his eyes. A spike of pain from his legs raced up his nervous system smashing into his brain. He squinted and rolled onto his side, away from the light.

Beside him stood a row of beds, each holding a man covered in white. An apparition finished snapping open the heavy drapes.

"Where am I?" he asked.

"Red Cross Hospital, in Milan. You were quite a mess when you arrived."

Rising to one elbow, he tore off the sheet, and was greatly relieved to see he still had both feet and all ten toes.

"Who are you?" he croaked out.

"Your nurse, Agnes, of the Red Cross," she responded, handing him a cool glass of water.

He took it with his right hand while still holding her hand against the glass with his left. He paused to drink in her beauty.

"Kind of a blow to your invincibility, isn't it?"

The voice came from the next bed over. From the uniform on a hanger above it, the lieutenant could see that his wardmate was also an officer of the Ambulance Corps.

"I'm Henry Villard." The man reached a hand across the aisle.

Taking the glass from Agnes, the lieutenant also reached out. "Ernest Hemingway."

"Well, Ernest, you are the talk of the ward."

"Why?"

Henry reached over and shook Hemingway's pillow, making a silver medal jump. "Italian Silver Medal of Bravery. A very fancy general pinned it there last night. Seems the boys you brought back from the front were very grateful."

Hemingway tried to focus on the medal, but it was too close. He looked up instead at a smiling Agnes, still backlit by the morning sun.

* * *

They made love to the tolling of the bell. Six months had passed, and for most of those months they had been together—lovers caught in a dichotomy of pain and ecstasy, passion and… guilt. He was here, and just a few miles away his comrades huddled in the snake, waiting to be digested.

As he leaned against the pillow, she handed him a cigarette and a glass of wine. "You should not feel ashamed of happiness."

"When the war is over, I won't."

She lit a cigarette for herself and replied, "Yes you will, because many will not go home."

He knew she was right. "In this world, there is good and bad, Agnes. Righteous and evil. In the Orient they call it 'yin and yang.'"

She grabbed him playfully. "Well, let's make the most of the hours we have left. I'll miss your 'yang' when it leaves tomorrow."

"It's only temporary. Your tour is up in two months, and then we'll be married in the States. We'll live a life of happiness for those who cannot."

"Yes, we will." She kissed him passionately.

PART I: THE YIN

CHAPTER 1

SOLDIER'S HOME

1919

A letter arrived instead of a bride. Agnes was engaged to an Italian officer.

Devastated, Hemingway retreated to his parents' cabin on Lake Waloon. His temporary pension—because of his wounds—allowed him to withdraw. Though only twenty years old, he had already seen more than most men would in a lifetime. Daily life and its pettiness seemed ridiculous after the epic struggle he had witnessed. Had *experienced*. How could his friends or family understand? They couldn't, of course—and he had no desire to try and explain.

His high school friends showed up one day and convinced him—more like kidnapped him—to go camping with them in Michigan's

Upper Peninsula. In the UP, September days were warm and nights cool. Hemingway marveled at the beauty—such a contrast to the sights and sounds that rang in his head in the form of memories. Here, he could whisk the dark images away by merely opening his eyes to the grandeur of nature. A soft sun caressed his face; a gentle breeze on a cloudless day whispered optimism in his ear; fuzz on the turning leaves massaged the back of his hand. Here, he was healed. Not cured, but healed.

He found himself addressing the Ladies Auxiliary not long after. His talk was riveting. Soon he was giving speeches and talks in uniform, medals shining, the epitome of masculinity. He thought it ridiculous and felt the ever-present tinge of guilt even as he regaled his audience. He wanted to be a writer, but his skill, his true essence, was as a story teller. In print or person didn't matter. In fact, he was so good at storytelling that a family friend demanded her husband get him a job at one of the newspapers in which he held a financial interest.

And thus began the next phase in Ernest Hemingway's life.

* * *

A light snow fell in the midmorning light, each tiny flake illuminated like a shooting star as it streaked past the window of the train before mixing with locomotive smoke and swirling away. Ernest Hemingway was on his way to Toronto to take a job as a freelance writer and foreign correspondent for the *Toronto Star Weekly*. He wasn't looking forward to the Great White North—he didn't like the cold—but his pension had run out, and he had nothing else.

* * *

It was clear that his new editor was not impressed. He scoffed at his experience and dismissed his war record as fantasy. A few weeks later, he stood at the exit of his hotel watching as the frigid wind whipped the snow through the gray streets. Pulling up his collar, he stepped into the revolving door, and pushed against the wind.

Hemingway marched into the *Star*'s offices in full uniform, his medals reflecting the overhead light. He banged through the door of his editor's glass office, and all eyes were on him as he hiked a foot on the editorial desk and yanked up his pant leg, revealing the wounds of war.

Saying nothing, Hemingway turned and left.

In June of the following year, he fled to his beloved Michigan and then settled in at the *Cooperative Commonwealth Journal* in Chicago.

CHAPTER 2

CROSS-COUNTRY SNOW

1920

Monotonous months passed, each day like a flake of snow. Different, but from a distance the same. He could feel the weight of the building snow crushing the life out of him. He was adrift, just going with the current, no course set. Strangely, he longed to be back on the Italian Front. Back to the life-and-death struggle. Back to every fiber of his being electrified, horrified, *alive*.

"You are in hell, aren't you?"

Hemingway looked up and met eyes with Sherwood Anderson, his co-worker.

"Is it that obvious?" he said.

"Yes, it is. I've fought my own demons, Ernest. I left them behind to become a writer…"

"I don't consider this writing, Sherwood."

"True. But you have to pay the bills."

"Cuba?"

"Excuse me?"

"Your demons. The war in Cuba?"

Sherwood laughed. "Oh my, no. By the time my company got to the island it was all over. In fact, I rather liked Cuba." He paused and smiled in reminiscence. "No, my demons came from being a successful businessman. I was being smothered, absolutely suffocated, by the bourgeoisie life. I had to escape and write. Quite literally to regain my sanity."

Hemingway held his eyes. "You're published. Why stay here?"

Again Sherwood laughed. "I told you, to pay the bills. Writing is a noble profession, and novels are the high wire. To create, in your own mind, a story and then put it onto paper is exhilarating. And the feeling of being deemed worthy of publication... it's beyond description. Euphoria. But it's also dangerous. It lays your soul bare; you submit to ridicule. And..."

He looked away to a distant point and smiled sadly.

"And you have to pay the bills," Hemingway finished.

"Exactly. Ernest, let's go get a drink."

CHAPTER 3

IN ANOTHER COUNTRY

1920

The warehouse district was just a few blocks away from the office. Sherwood banged on a steel door in a non-descript alley, and a narrow slot clicked open, exposing only two eyes.

"Password?" the menacing green eyes demanded.

"Red dog."

Metal bolts retracted, their action sounding like a rifle chambering a round—a comfortable sound to Hemingway, and the door opened.

They stepped into a dark antechamber. The door behind them was re-latched, then the inner door to the sanctum opened. Music, smoke, and the smell of booze filled their senses. As their pupils dilated, dim lights on tables slowly revealed a speakeasy. A band blasted out a tune Hemingway had heard on the radio that morning, and a line of flappers high-kicked provocatively across the dance floor, their beaded outfits swung in rhythm in a delightfully revealing way.

As Hemingway and Sherwood took a seat, a waitress appeared out of the dim light, dressed like the dancers, and set an ashtray in front of them. Hemingway struck a match violating the dark sanctum. Its light flickered in her eyes; they flirted without a word being said.

They ordered their drinks, and the waitress departed.

"So," Sherwood said. "What is it you want?"

"Besides her?"

"In addition to her."

Hemingway took a long drag off his cigarette, exhaling blue smoke that disappeared as it moved outside the illumination of their table. Leaning back in contemplation, he raised his voice over the band.

"I want what I thought I had: the love of a good wife and an exciting life of writing."

"Ah. A broken heart is on your list of wounds."

Hemingway shrugged and said nothing.

Sherwood shook out a cigarette, tapped it once on the table, and lit it with a fancy silver lighter. Then leaning in close he said, "Use it."

Hemingway met his intense glare.

"Use all of it. Write what you know. What you felt. What you lived. Authenticity. People, your readers, want to be scintillated. They want to be excited, enticed by the forbidden fruit. Look around you: Were there ever women in the pubs before prohibition? Rich people? No. But now? The speakeasies are full of both, because it's exciting, it's taboo. Give your readers the fruit in the form of the written word. Take them where they secretly want to go."

For months, the two men continued their dialogue at the Red Dog. They discussed life, current events, women, but always circled back to writing. And in that time Sherwood became not only Hemingway's mentor, but also a trusted friend.

* * *

Hemingway stood in front of a mirror trying to straighten his tie. A cool lake breeze blew the white linen curtains and filled the room with spring.

A soft knock sounded on the door.

Annoyed, he crossed the room and yanked open the door expecting to see the irritating superintendent. Instead, two fetching young women stood in the hallway.

His roommate entered the living room and invited the two women in. One was his sister; the other, an auburn-haired beauty, was named Hadley. Hemingway was instantly smitten with the latter. She giggled and straightened his tie.

"Ladies, may I introduce Ernest Hemingway, war hero and aspiring writer."

Hemingway tuned out everyone and everything except Hadley. They sat on a loveseat in front of a window, caressed by the soft breeze, and talked for hours. His plans for the night were cast aside. He talked of Europe and his aspirations for the future; she spoke of her desire to escape an overbearing mother. Like Agnes she was older than him. Unlike Agnes, she was less worldly and more gregarious.

Hemingway felt empty when she left for St Louis. They began an intense liaison by mail. A shared goal of escape flowed through the letters: he wanted to escape a life of tedium, she wanted to escape a life with her mother. For both of them, Europe was the promised land.

In early September of 1921 they joined forces and were married.

* * *

"Rome, Sherwood, Rome!" cried Hemingway. He and Hadley sat with Sherwood in the Red Dog, detailing their plan of expatriation.

"How will you two live?" Sherwood asked.

"The *Toronto Star* has hired me as a foreign correspondent, and Hadley has a small trust fund."

Sherwood shook his head and stage-whispered for effect: "Paris, my young friends. Paris!"

"Why?"

"Two reasons. First, it is where you will embrace and learn your craft. Paris is drawing a vibrant new generation of writers, artists, and free thinkers. You simply *must* go to Paris."

"What is the second reason?"

"The exchange rate, because…"

All three laughed as they chanted, "You have to pay the bills."

* * *

Union Station bustled with activity—activity that Hemingway watched intently. He had taken out a small notebook and was jotting down observations to be used later in a story.

Sherwood smiled and pulled a flask from an inner suit coat pocket. He poured a shot into each of their coffees.

"I wish I was going with you two."

"Why don't you?" Hemingway said.

"Yes, Sherwood, join us," Hadley added.

"No. This is your journey."

He returned the flask and produced a letter from the same pocket, handing it to Hemingway.

"What's this?"

"A letter of introduction, to Gertrude Stein."

"*The* Gertrude Stein?" Hemingway met Hadley's eyes, and she smiled back excitedly.

"Yes, *the* Gertrude. You will find her at the Stein Salon, 27 Rue de Fleurus. Go on Saturday evening. It is the unofficial clubhouse of the Lost Generation."

"Who is the Lost Generation?"

"You, my dear boy. Now. Time to board your train."

Steam rolled down the platform, undisturbed by breeze, consuming an engineer to his waist. The man floated disembodied on the cloud, and as Hemingway watched, it sent a chill down his spine.

Hadley tugged him onto the last train car, the observation car. Her enthusiasm was infectious, and she overpowered his sudden melancholy as she sat beside him in a rear-facing seat.

The locomotive inched forward, easing out of the station, slowly building up steam.

"I can't wait to see the Eiffel Tower," Hadley gushed.

Black smoke fluttered around their car, and bright sunlight flashed down from the small windows overhead as they emerged from the train shed. But even as they moved forward into the light, Hemingway was drawn to the dark shadows of the station behind them.

CHAPTER 4

THE LIGHT OF THE WORLD

1922

Paris. The City of Light. The city of optimism. The city of enlightenment and the future. The yin. Full of artists, sculptors, writers, and free thinkers, all spun off of the nucleus of destruction that was the Great War.

They were a lost generation, one that could not un-see what they had seen when the world was plunged into chaos and horror. They came to Paris, where they painted, wrote, and drank away their physical and spiritual wounds. It was a time of beauty and truth. Art, literature and freedom filled the air. Anything was possible.

By contrast, Berlin had fallen into darkness. Made to pay for the sins of the war by the victorious Allies, Germany could not escape the chaos. Instead it plunged deeper. Turning on itself; morose, depressed, self-loathing.

A destroyed economy fueled heinous crime, Germany showed all the symptoms of a failing civilization. Even the cabarets were dour and depressing; instead of an air of gaiety, they provided only an underlying feeling of peril.

If Paris was the yin, Berlin was the yang. It was the epicenter of another spiral into the abyss.

Light fades to dark slowly, Madrid was somewhere between—in twilight. Being pulled from light to dark as Spain stumbled slowly toward civil war.

It was in this continental arena that the Lost Generation tried to create. Tried to make a positive mark on a damaged world. They were the optimists, the citizens of light, fighting against the dark, trying to make sense of it all.

Hemingway flowered during this time. Gertrude introduced him to Pablo Picasso, he ran into Ezra Pound at the bookstore Shakespeare and Company, and he was becoming a full member of Gertrude's Lost Generation—along with F. Scott Fitzgerald, Sinclair Lewis, Gavin Williamson, Thornton Wilder, Sherwood Anderson, Henri Matisse, and many more.

Hemingway and Hadley moved into 74 Rue du Cardinal Lemoine, and he began to churn out material in his small studio next door. He worked hard by day, and loved his time meeting with members of the Lost Generation for happy hour. It was an exciting time.

La Dome, in the Montparnasse section of Paris, was one of the favorites of the Lost Generation members. Long conversations were laced with whiskey and wine and went late into the evenings. Smoke curled from ashtrays up to the yellowed ceiling above. Spring air from an open door would try to push it away, but failed. Gertrude would hold court in the bright light, discussing world events and writing. Mostly writing, for this group had surrendered to its power totally. And Hemingway was usually at her side; he had clearly become the favorite son.

Soon Hemingway was taking over the conversation, handsome, larger than life, reading aloud from his latest work. His writing elevated souls, quenched a thirst, and crushed a competitor's will.

But an evil swirled in the room, as present as the smoke. Palpable to only one. It was envy—a coveting. A lust for what was not possessed, but was close enough to touch, to feel, to read. Hatred was simmering to a boil, seething at Hemingway's every word.

CHAPTER 5

ON THE QUAI AT SMYRNA

1922

E ven living in the City of Light, Hemingway felt pulled to the dark. And so it was that September found him chugging through the Balkan Mountains on the Orient Express, headed back to war. This time as an observer—a foreign war correspondent.

After crushing the Greeks at Afyon, Mustafa "Atatürk" Kemal fell upon Smyrna. Greek invaders poured onto ships to escape the disastrous campaign, but there were not enough for civilians—and then the city was set on fire by the Turks.

The mutual hatred between the Greeks and Turks went back millennia. Religion, culture, and shifting borders created an animus kept alive by long memories. Rape, pillage, and plunder, torn from the tenth century, now raged through the twentieth.

This was what had obligated Hemingway to journey to Constantinople.

From the balcony of the Buyuk Londres Hotel, he gazed across Constantinople. Dirty white spires rose from the mosques, and dust hung over everything, kicked into the air by feet, tires, anything that moved. The tension rose from the streets like heat from the sun. Atatürk was waiting to take the city, whose citizens were already painfully aware of what had happened in Smyrna.

Hemingway scratched at the insect bites on his face and wiped the blood from his arms, drawn by the bed bugs. Stale air hung over the city, filled with putrid smells, it was so still the odors could not dissipate. He wondered who would fight to the death for such a place.

He walked down the dirty steps of the hotel. On the sidewalk, its owner stood armed to the teeth, determined to protect his property. Hemingway nodded at the man as he stepped out into the dust.

Rats scurried past, wretched dogs picked at garbage in the gutters, an old man lay dead in an alley decomposing. Hemingway pressed on as the call for prayer rang out from the minarets. Ahead he could see the neon sign of a dive bar. He checked his notebook for the name he had scrawled into it.

He stepped into the bar. Smoke filled the room from his knees up, dusting his khaki pants. He tried in vain to brush it off.

Looking around the room, he spotted a man chain smoking and drinking what appeared to be a gin and tonic. Hemingway walked over to him.

"You already have one lit." Hemingway pointed to half a cigarette smoldering in the ash tray.

"So I do, so I do. Hemingway?" the man asked in a British accent.

Hemingway nodded and sat down. "You were in Smyrna?"

"Yes, and damn glad to be back to civilization."

Hemingway raised an eyebrow at the comment.

"Where you in the Great War, Hemingway?"

"Yes. The trenches on the Italian Front."

The man nodded distantly. "A damn garden party…"

Hemingway waited for an explanation.

"They screamed every night, Hemingway. Usually around midnight. It was the damnedest thing."

"Who?"

"The women, and the old."

"Then what?"

The man drank from his dirty glass and took a long drag from his vulgar Turkish cigarette. Narrowing his eyes, he looked directly at Hemingway.

"One of the ship's mates would shine a spotlight on them."

"And?"

"They would quit. Damnedest thing."

"Are you drunk? You're not making much sense."

"Not yet, sadly. I suppose I should start from the top."

"Please."

"Yes, well. I was in my hotel, a nasty little dump, when the Turks lit the city ablaze. They used petrol, so it moved quickly. I went downstairs to the bar, tapped a spoon on an ice bucket, and announced the city was alight. We gathered, the few of us left, and commandeered a truck. It was a bit of a harrowing drive. Like everyone else in the city, we headed for the main pier. Our credentials got us aboard a vessel, and we anchored out a bit. Unfortunately, there were not enough ships. Thousands were left on the pier, no water or food…"

The man looked at the ember of his cigarette, fixating on it.

"The city burned…"

"And then?"

"Life and death… Mothers gave birth, while others clutched dead babies to their breasts. Dead, bloated animals floated in the bay. Old people were next. The city burned."

Hemingway closed his notebook and picked up the glass of whiskey a fat disheveled waiter had left him.

"Have you ever smelled a burning body, Hemingway?"

Hemingway paused with the whiskey to his lips, then took a swig. "Yes."

"Rather unpleasant, isn't it?"

CHAPTER 6

HOMAGE TO SWITZERLAND

December 1922

The Conference of Lausanne in Switzerland ended when the Turks boarded the Orient Express and went home. Hemingway was on assignment for the *Toronto Star* at the time, working on a draft while sipping a martini in the Beau-Rivage Palace Hotel's bar.

Snow drifted down, covering the lawn with a fresh coat of white. He watched it through the plate glass window. Beyond the lawn, it kissed the lake and disappeared.

Lincoln Steffens, an editor, sat down next to him. He waved over a perfectly dressed and manicured waiter and ordered a martini for him and another for Hemingway.

"So, what did you think of Mussolini's speech, Ernest?"

"Blowhard fascist."

"You are not worried about them?"

"Actually, I'm quite sure they will blow up the world again. But does that ever stop?"

"No, I suppose it doesn't. Why is that, do you think?"

"Yin and yang. Good and evil. That struggle is in each of us. It is the nature of mankind. Technology has just made it more effective, and horrific. But it hasn't changed since Cain killed Abel."

"I read that in your work, Ernest."

"Well Lincoln, I didn't know you cared," Hemingway said jokingly.

Lincoln laughed. "I'd love to read more, for publication. Do you have any of your manuscripts here?"

"No, but I will by tomorrow night." Hemingway waved the waiter over. "My good man, I need to send a telegram."

* * *

Hadley was having lunch with Gertrude at Le Dome, but the gray December day had driven them from their sidewalk table. As they re-settled at a table inside, a Western Union boy walked in, calling her name.

"I'm Madame Hemingway."

He handed her a telegram and left before she could tip him. Nervously, she tore it open and read it.

"What is it, dear?"

A huge smile erupted on Hadley's face. She handed Gertrude the telegram.

"This is very good news!" Gertrude said. "Take all his work. This could be a breakthrough."

"He booked me on the noon train tomorrow."

"Perfect. Then there is time."

"For what?"

Gertrude clapped her hands over her head once. A waiter rushed over.

"Garçon, a bottle of champagne!"

Across the room, but within earshot, envy boiled over.

CHAPTER 7

THE TRAIN RIDE

He was a petty man. An evil man. But even in his evilness, he was petty. A thief. But a slothful one. He was unable to achieve any lofty goal or worthwhile accomplishment even as a criminal. He stole only bits and pieces from those that had.

Jean Paul Arnott pulled up his soiled collar against the dark mist that rolled off the Seine. He watched as a figure emerged from the fog, walking with an arrogance worn like the overcoat that hung from his rounded shoulders.

"You are clear on your instructions?"

"Very."

"Good. Remember, his wife will be alone. It should be a simple task to—"

"Do not tell me how to do my job, and I will not tell you how to write." Cold eyes looked from under a fedora. "Yes, I know who you are."

"Just get the suitcase and meet me in front of Notre Dame tomorrow at three o'clock sharp."

*   *   *

The clock tower of the Gare de Lyon Train Station struck the half hour as Hadley hurried past. It was large, fashioned after Big Ben in London, and was quite out of place in Paris.

Inside the station, Hadley entered Le Train Bleu, where she found a table near the artwork of Albert Maignan. With the heavy suitcase tucked safely under the table, she ordered a sandwich and a bottle of Evian water. But service was quite slow, so she wrapped the sandwich in a newspaper and hauled the suitcase into the great hall to hail a porter. He got her on board and put the suitcase next to her seat.

Hadley suddenly realized she had forgotten her bottle of water. She exited the train and walked quickly back to Le Train Bleu. Her water was still on the table where she'd left it. She grabbed it and rushed back to the train.

*   *   *

In the locomotive, an engineer read the steam pressure gauge and vented the excess. A cloud grew on the platform as Arnott stepped off the train with Hemingway's suitcase in hand. Hadley was hurrying down the platform, but Arnott walked into the growing steam cloud and disappeared.

An easy score, a theft of another man's work. Heart and soul laid bare on paper, and he'd snatched it away like it was no more than an apple. He didn't care; he was a petty and slothful man who could not comprehend its significance.

34

CHAPTER 8

TO HAVE AND HAVE NOT

Hemingway sat slumped over a very stiff whiskey in the hotel bar, a crumpled telegram in the ashtray. Picasso had joined him that day, confused that he hadn't seen Hadley on the train, until he too read the message from her. He now sat silently, consoling his friend for the loss.

"She even put in the carbon copies, Pablo. Why would you do that?"

"You must guard against blaming her, Ernest. It is the thief who is at fault."

Hemingway nodded absently and guzzled the whiskey. Then he slammed the glass on the table and bellowed.

"I curse the evil that steals my words! I curse it to a fate of itself! An eye for an eye. An evil for evil!"

Picasso spoke calmly. "Kind of a petty crime to unleash a curse of such epic proportions, don't you think?"

Hemingway raised his glass high so the waiter could see it was empty. "Evil knows no boundary," he said. "Small or large, it is the same beast. It lives, breeds, and gains strength in insignificant deeds even more than great acts, because the petty acts are done just for the sake of cruelty."

A sudden melancholy swept him into the future. A deep fissure opened in his soul for an instant—and then closed.

A fresh whiskey was set down on the table. Hemingway picked it up and looked at it as if seeing for the first time in his life. The storm cleared from his eyes.

"This will be both my savior and tormentor."

He held it up and looked past Picasso at an old woman who had been clearing a table but was now riveted on Hemingway. Her hair was white, tied in a tight long braid, and her dark eyes were cutting. A gypsy.

Hemingway waved her over. As she stood before him, he rifled through his attaché case. Finally, he produced a photograph of him and Hadley arriving in Paris, standing in front of the Eiffel Tower. At his feet sat the suitcase.

"You're a damn gypsy," Hemingway said. "Put a curse on this."

"Ernest," Picasso said. "Enough."

Hemingway folded the picture so it showed only him and the suitcase. He tapped on the suitcase.

"Put a curse on it, you old dumb bitch," he demanded

The woman's eyes flared red, but she said nothing. Instead pointing to him in the picture. Hemingway slammed a twenty-dollar gold piece on the table, tore the picture in half horizontally, and threw the lower half at her.

A second flare erupted from her dark eyes. She picked up the torn photo, looked at it, his legs still visible, then shrugged.

"It is your curse too, even if by half," she whispered in a thick Hungarian accent.

Picasso squirmed nervously in his chair.

The gypsy woman reached behind her white linen apron and produced a well-worn, dark red leather bag. She shook it twice over the picture, then opened it and dropped a pinch of spice or powder of some kind on the suitcase in the photograph. Her incantation was barely audible.

Finally she crossed her arms, apparently finished.

Hemingway grabbed it spreading the dust across the entire picture. "That's it?"

"That is more than enough."

The woman turned to Picasso and took his hand. Her grip was strong but soft. Smiling, she whispered, "To you, a blessing."

"A blessing of what, Grandmother?"

"Of beauty without boundary or form. Unlimited beauty." She took a small flower from her bag and handed it to him.

"Thank you, Grandmother."

She left quietly and strode confidently away.

"What now, Ernest?"

Hemingway held up his whiskey. Picasso raised his as well. They clinked them with authority and drank.

"To hell with that suitcase, Pablo. It is gone."

"I hope so," Picasso mumbled under his breath.

CHAPTER 9

THE KILLERS

A light snow fell on Paris, barely an inch had gathered on the pavement in front of Notre Dame. Arnott crunched softly through it on his way to the main entrance, the heavy suitcase in his hand.

Envy watched his approach.

Envy was not the only one. Across the square, Inspector Richard recognized the thief Arnott—and paid particular attention to the suitcase. Alligator leather, very nice… definitely not Arnott's. The inspector decided to shake down Arnott, because he was a corrupt policeman and, like Arnott, an evil man.

Arnott saw the inspector moving toward him. He bolted. Richard gave chase.

Envy looked on in disbelief as Arnott slipped and fell in front of a bus. Unable to stop in the snow, the bus ran him over.

A crowd gathered around the crushed man. Richard flashed a badge and ordered them back.

"Jean Paul, what do you have for me here?" he whispered. He pried Arnott's fingers from around the suitcase's handle.

Arnott tried to curse him with his last breath, but only coughed blood. Around him, the snow had turned bright red. A compound fracture of his femur had nicked an artery.

"You should have just given it to me, Jean Paul," Richard taunted.

A priest pushed his way through the crowd, past envy. He went down on one knee and made the sign of the cross, ready to administer last rites.

Arnott bled out and died. Richard felt nothing for the man. No one would; he had been an evil and petty man.

At one time Richard had been a good man, but that time had passed long ago. He had been corrupted not despite his position but because of it. Weak, he simply could not resist the temptation to take advantage of the timid and steal from criminals. On the streets, he was feared for his brutality and his penchant for tortured confessions. This gave him an impressive case record, which caused his superiors to look the other way.

He was alone when he opened Hemingway's suitcase. He rifled through the manuscripts and carbons. Mere papers? He grew frustrated and slammed it shut.

But Richard was shrewd. Arnott had died trying to escape with this—which meant these papers had value. Somebody would surface, or perhaps a reward would be offered in the newspaper. He could get his brother to claim it. Until then he would tag it as special evidence, with his name on it and marked *do not remove.*

Inspector Richard walked silently down the steps. A fresh blanket of snow muffled the city. He walked through the fog of his breath to a local bistro. After two meals and a fine bottle of wine he walked away without paying—as always. He flashed his badge and a sneer on the way out. He was smart enough to spread his larceny around; he never preyed upon the same establishment too often.

Feeling good from the gratis wine, he moved on to his favorite bar—The Loading Dock, a seedy little dump near the river. For now, white snow sanitized even this part of Paris. But by mid-morning the trucks and vans that filled the barges would soil it.

Filthy light seeped from the bar as Richard' struggled to get his fat body through the partially open door.

The smoky air inside the bar smelled of vomit and urine, with a hint of crime. Richard felt at home with the criminal element, even though he preyed on them. He pushed a passed-out drunk off a barstool and onto the slimy floor. Taking the now-vacant seat, he demanded a whiskey.

Wrath watched him from a dark corner, motionless. Empty eyes took in the surroundings, scanning, plotting, desiring revenge. A drink was pushed away, a plan formulated. Fueled by adrenaline, all senses came alive in anticipation.

In the distance, a clock tower tolled twice. Richard pulled out a gold pocket watch he had lifted from a heart attack victim years before. He clicked it open, smirked at some loving wife's inscription, and tried to focus through drunken eyes. Snapping it shut, he slapped some dirty francs on the bar and left.

Wrath stalked him from the shadows. His hooded overcoat was embraced by the night, concealing him. He was silent motion born of purpose, hunting in the pure night.

Richard wobbled, his brain swimming in alcohol. He grabbed the pole of a streetlight to steady himself. Leaning over, he puked on the snow and his feet.

A switchblade's click announced danger as loudly as a claxon, breaking through to his whiskey-addled brain. His reflexes, however, could not respond. Wrath pounced from its sanctuary into the dim light and buried six inches of stiletto deep into Richard's fat neck.

"Remember me, Richard?"

Dying eyes opened wide, but not with recognition. There had been so many.

In an abrupt, violent movement, revenge was extracted. Blood sprayed from Richard's throat, sent forth by a racing and cold heart.

Dead eyes stared into nothing. Wrath released Richard's collar and let his body crumple into the vomit. His lifeless head hit the curb with an awkward twist as his blood drained into the gutter.

CHAPTER 10

AFTER THE STORM

Hemingway wrote with a fury, as if in a race to get his stories published before they could be lost. This resulted in two things: a change in his style—his impatience to get a manuscript finished could be seen in his clipped words and compact structure—and a prolific amount of material.

The crystal-clear water of the Irati River ran through a small valley in the Pyrenees, outside the tiny village of Aribe. Hemingway stood thigh deep in the frigid current that kept him cool on the hot humid day. Gentle waters of the Irati River flowed around him, as he whipped a handmade fly over its surface three times with a bamboo pole before letting it settle on top of a swirling pool. Instantly, a trout struck it. Realizing it was a trap, the fish dove to escape, but

Hemingway raised the pole's tip to keep the proper amount of tension on the line so the fish couldn't spit the hook. He relished the battle, a life and death struggle for the trout.

He reeled in a bit of slack each time the fish moved toward him. If it wanted to run, he let it; it would only tire the fish out and lengthen the fight. He was winning, and both he and the fish knew it. Yet it fought on courageously.

Even the brave weakened—and Hemingway felt it. Gently, out of respect for his noble opponent, he reeled the fish in. He held the pole high with one hand until he could grab the fish by its gill. He did not use a net; he considered it an unfair advantage.

Carefully, to cause it no pain, he eased the hook out of the great trout's gasping mouth. As he placed the fish in a wicker basket that hung on his hip, Hemingway felt the last of its feeble efforts to escape.

"I shall eat you first, brave fish."

He felt no pity, just as the fish had felt none for the fly. It was nature's order.

Hemingway waded over to Enrique, who had watched all this from the shade of a pine tree. The two of them headed down a narrow goat trail and across the Irati on an ancient stone bridge. Its three arches delivered them to the heart of Aribe.

Hemingway paused to observe a new road being cut into the side of a mountain. "Are you happy to be finally getting a good road, Enrique?"

Enrique shook his head sadly. "Good roads bring bad people."

Hemingway fell silent, contemplating highwaymen, desperadoes, and armies on the march. Enrique was right: good roads did indeed bring bad people to places like this.

It was in these days that Hemingway drifted to and from Hadley. An unnamed force had invaded their relationship—the suitcase—yet each continued to try. Hemingway traveled throughout Europe and wrote stories of his exploits. Ezra Pound became a close friend, and James Joyce, introduced by Ezra, became a drinking partner. A *hard* drinking partner.

Hadley announced she was pregnant one afternoon before Hemingway went out with Joyce. Thrust into a sudden, heavy responsibility, he was forced to consider their financial future. The ensuing months were filled with rushing together his first book: *Three Stories and Ten Poems.*

*   *   *

Hemingway and Hadley went to Pamplona, Spain, for a bullfight in late summer. Round and steep, the stadium was packed with cheering Spaniards. Hadley was uncomfortable at being jostled, and sat quietly as Hemingway joined with the boisterous crowd.

A parade of the matador's *cuadrilla*, his team, strode past in colorful eighteenth-century Andalusian costumes. Their *traje de luces* glistened in the hot summer sky. One was embroidered with silver, the other in gold. Two *picadores*, lancers, were mounted on horseback. Three *banderilleros* on foot waved their magenta and gold *capotes*. Each cape moved as if it were solid, not made of cloth. A *mozo de espada* followed each matador as his sword servant.

A trumpet announced the first stage of the fight: the *terico de varas*, the part of lancers. Adorned in his silver suit, the first matador watched as his *banderilleros* got him to charge their *capos*.

"Look, Hadley," Hemingway said. "No, not at the *banderil-leros*—watch the matador. See how he is evaluating the bull? How it charges and thrusts, where it goes. See how it's backed into a spot in the ring?"

She nodded nervously as the bull scraped at the dirt with a hoof.

"That is his territory in the ring, his *querencia*, and where he is the most dangerous."

Moving forward in *suerte de capote*, the matador taunted with his footwork and cape, inviting attack. Intricate movements of the cape incited the bull. When he let it drag over the charging bull's head as it passed, he was rewarded with loud chants from the crowd.

"*Olé, olé, olé!*"

"That movement is called the *verónica*," Hemingway explained.

Horses thundered into the ring with their *picadors* on their backs, armed with lances. The first *picador* scored only a glancing blow on the bull's neck. The bull twisted with incredible speed and gored the horse in its belly.

Shrieks from the dying horse filled the air as the matador demanded the attention of the bull. It charged him while the *picador* struggled free of the downed horse.

The second *picador* streaked past the matador after the bull's pass, and drove a lance into the bull's neck. As he continued his charges against the bull, he was careful not to make the mistake his fellow *picador* had made. This bull was a ferocious beast, snorting blood and pawing at the dirt, and was anxious to inflict its own wounds. But each cut in the bull's neck caused his head to hang a little lower.

A trumpet blast announced the *tercio de banderillas*.

Three *banderilleros* rushed into the ring, each with two barbed sticks adorned with colored paper in the local province's colors. They stabbed their sticks into the bull's neck as they passed, in an effort to further weaken the animal.

Hemingway could see that the bull retained the bulk of its strength, but unfortunately, the *presidente* of the corrida appeared not to, as he ordered the final stage: the *tercio de muerte*. The part of death.

The trumpet sounded and the ring cleared, leaving only the bull.

A second blow of the trumpet announced the matador's re-emer-gence, this time alone. He held his cape and a sword in one hand as he moved toward the bull's *querencia*.

"Now are the *tondas*," Hemingway said. "A series of dramatic passes. This is where the matador shows what he has!"

"It's so brutal."

"Yes, it is. It will toughen up our son." He gave Hadley a wide smile, patted her on the belly, and turned back to the life-and-death struggle. The crowd chanted, the bull charged, blood flowed. After a particularly close and grandiose wave of the cape, the crowd went wild.

"That was a *pase de desprecio*! Now is the time for *estoque*."

Hadley didn't need to ask what that was—the matador already held the sword out, point down, as the bull charged the cape. At the last second it veered and caught the matador by the thigh, tossing him into the air, head over heel.

Hemingway sighed. "The bull won."

A sword stuck out of the top of the bull's shoulder, sun glinted off the blade. The crowd went silent.

Banderilleros stormed into the ring and distracted the bull, giving the matador time. He rose unsteadily to his feet, his silver-emblazoned pant leg torn open to reveal a large wound. He raised his hat in salute and left the ring.

The *presidente* ordered a parade lap for the bull, and then it was ushered out of the ring by the *banderilleros*. The crowd cheered loudly.

"What now, Ernest?"

"He gets to live."

"Can we go now?"

"There is another fight. After that we can leave."

Hemingway pulled out his notebook and took extensive notes as the second corrida started. It had the same schedule of events, but the gold matador and his *cuadrilla* were obviously much more experienced. The fight was without flaw, and ended when the matador plunged a sword to the hilt between the bull's shoulder blades on its last pass. Delighted by the performance, the presidente presented the matador one of the bull's ears.

The jubilant crowd lifted the victorious matador on their shoulders and carried him from the ring. The bull, meanwhile, was dragged from the ring by horses, leaving a dark trail of blood behind it.

Hadley pointed toward a priest who stood near the open gate. "What is he here for?" she asked.

Hemingway looked up from his notes. "Last rites, and not for the bull. And he gets the meat for his orphanage."

"Ernest, I want to go home for the birth of our baby."

CHAPTER 11

MEN WITHOUT WOMEN

1923

His studies hadn't ended abruptly—they had just faded away. Like his writing, which had eroded until he was staring at blank pages. At twenty, his life seemed over. No prospects. No future. Glancing around the beer hall, he realized that this might be it.

He lifted the mop out of the bucket, twirled it, and let it flop on the floor. Water went everywhere, making the mess of spilled beer worse.

"You must wring it out first."

He turned to face a man with hard eyes and a peculiar little mustache.

"You don't see yourself a custodian, do you?"

"No," he answered. "I wanted to be a writer."

"And I a painter. Perhaps destiny holds something different for both of us. What is your name?"

"Johan Schrict."

"Join us, Johan."

"Who?"

"The Socialist Party of Germany. We intend to rebuild the Fatherland."

Johan noted the brown shirt and sleeve band. He nodded to the band. "What is that?"

"Our party's symbol. Stay tonight and listen."

Johan nodded enthusiastically as he wrung out the mop.

CHAPTER 12

THE TRADESMAN'S RETURN

1924

Hemingway was bored in Toronto. His first book had been published and a few months later, another followed. He felt that he was finally a legitimate writer and wanted to leave his journalist life behind. And he missed Paris.

His newly expanded family journeyed back to Paris in early 1924. He worked on his novel, *The Sun Also Rises*, and as an editor for the *Transatlantic Review*, where he published his friends' stories and a few of his own.

Trips to Pamplona were monumental. In fact, he would eventually pick up the nickname Papa, short for Pamplona. And after a trip in 1925, he would pick up a new champion as well.

When Pauline Pfeiffer joined them in Pamplona, Hadley sensed she was a threat. Pauline urged Hemingway to sign with Scribner Publishing; Hadley was against it. When he signed, she knew it was over. Hemingway began an affair with Pauline. Hadley withdrew into herself.

She and Hemingway had grown further apart even before Pauline, and she knew why: the suitcase. It had always been the suitcase. She cursed it in her dark times. The affair was simply the excuse she needed to end the pain. She and Hemingway were divorced in January of 1927.

The Sun Also Rises was published to great reviews and success. Hemingway gave the royalties to Hadley, and she and their son Jack moved back to the States. Hemingway had gained the writing success he had worked so hard for, but had lost his family.

Men Without Women was published the following fall. It was a collection of short stories, including the boxing story "Fifty Grand," one of his best. To make the story real, Hemingway even learned to box. He would continue to fight for many years, in and out of the ring, in and over himself.

Hemingway married Pauline. But they could not stay in Paris. To Hemingway, Paris was Hadley, even after she was gone. So they made the decision to leave the City of Light.

As they were packing, he came upon the torn picture of the lost suitcase. Hadley was gone. The suitcase was gone. Crushing the picture in his fist, he walked into the bathroom and tossed it into the toilet. He watched it sink as he reached up for the chain and yanked it.

His head erupted in pain, the room swirled, and he saw more stars than he ever had in the ring.

Down on one knee he pressed a hand to his forehead. He felt the warm blood. Keeping pressure on the wound, he looked up to see what had hit him. A skylight. He had yanked down the skylight, not flushed the toilet.

He got up on his feet, unsteady he struggled from the bathroom into the hall. Pauline screamed when she saw the blood. They rushed off to the hospital.

In the bathroom, the crumpled picture floated back to the surface and opened. The water around it turned a strange color of yellow, mixing with drops of Hemingway's dissipating blood.

Hemingway would visit the City of Light again, but he would never live there. It was Hadley's. Key West was his newfound home, and he loved it. It was a rough-and-tumble place, a fisherman's paradise. And best of all, it possessed scoundrels, sailors, pirates, and characters of all sorts to spark a writer's imagination.

CHAPTER 13

FATHERS AND SONS

1928

Hemingway's life was at a very happy point. His second son, Patrick, had been born in late spring, he was bringing his first son, Jack, to Florida, and his professional career was both profitable and critically acclaimed.

He and Jack were seated on a wooden bench, waiting to board their train, when a Western Union boy in full uniform held up a telegram and shouted a name that was drowned out by the public-address system. He repeated it a second time.

"Telegram for Mr. Ernest Hemingway."

People turned to look. Hemingway's name was becoming famous, especially in a city like New York.

"I'm Ernest Hemingway."

Hemingway took the cable and tipped the young man. He had a feeling of foreboding even before he read the message—a feeling that was proven well-founded. His father had committed suicide.

Hemingway was devastated. He rushed to a phone and called his mother.

"I sent a letter," he said. "I told him not to worry about finances."

"Yes, I know, Ernest. It came after he… it wasn't just finances."

"I know, I know."

* * *

Hemingway returned to Florida after the funeral. He worked on *A Farewell To Arms*, an effort that was interrupted by a trip to France—he needed to escape. But he returned to Key West and finished the novel before returning to Europe, this time to do research for *Death in the Afternoon*, a book on the life-and-death struggle of bullfighting.

Pauline's rich uncle, who loved Hemingway's work, had bought them a beautiful house. It had a porch and second-floor balcony that wrapped around the entire house. Four large windows on each wall ran from the floor almost to the ceiling, and all were rounded at the top. A maid's quarters were located over the garage, and Hemingway converted it to a writing studio. He had a cast-iron walkway installed that matched the balcony's railing. Every morning he would rise and cross to his writer's lair, where he would write all day. Every afternoon he was in his regulation boxing ring, and then down to Sloppy Joe's, or Red's, or even the Bucket of Blood.

Creation by light, mayhem in the darkness.

Financial independence came with the success of *A Farewell to Arms*. The Hemingway's began spending summers in Wyoming and winters in Key West. Even in Wyoming, he kept his routine: he would write in the mornings, but by midday it was blood sport. Hunting bear was his favorite, because if you failed, the hunter became the hunted.

CHAPTER 14

THE PORTER

1933

He was restless. He was flat. Even the bear hunts had become routine. They didn't satiate his lust for the struggle between life and death. The Wyoming hunts were pills, and he needed the needle. Hemingway felt his inspiration and motivation slipping away.

An ancient sun broke over the Serengeti. He watched as it awoke the flat plain. Giant siafu ants began to scurry on their metropolis of mud that stood twice as tall as a man. Birds took flight from the umbrella-shaped acacia trees, their black shapes flapping against an orange sky. Large animals made their way to the watering hole his party was bivouacked near.

A truce hung over each watering hole at sunrise and sunset. It was a sanctuary that would not extend to the rest of the Serengeti. All-out war would soon rage. Hunters and the hunted.

An eight-foot black mamba sprang from the underbrush, striking a Maasai warrior with such force it knocked him down. Its long fangs sank deep into the porter's side. Philip Percival pushed past Hemingway and slashed off its head with a machete.

But it was too late. Poison had already shot from the snake's glands into the doomed Porter's body. He writhed in pain and shock, pulling at the decapitated head of the viper. As his pounding heart carried the poison through his veins, he began to cough and then became paralyzed. Fear filled his eyes. He looked directly into Hemingway's for help.

Hemingway couldn't look away even as he spoke. "Do we have any antivenom, Philip?"

"I'm afraid not." Glancing at his watch he added, "It won't be long, old chap. It was a big one."

Hemingway knelt next to the man, transfixed by the inevitability, frustrated by the futility. Less than twenty minutes later the Maasai's breathing slowed and stopped. His fellow tribesmen moved in and mourned over him, beginning a death chant.

"Come along, Ernest," said Philip. "We will leave them to their ceremony. This is not for us. They will catch up to us later."

"Won't they take him back to the village for burial?"

"No. It is not the Maasai way. He will be left for the vulture and hyena."

Hemingway looked back at the warriors. They had formed a circle around the fallen man and were leaping in unison, spears at their sides. They didn't bend at the knees; they were propelled into the air by the power of their calves only. They were leaping amazingly high when Philip pulled him into the bush and out of sight.

They moved with a renewed caution toward the herd of Cape Buffalo. When Philip suddenly held his hand up and motioned to the ground beneath a low bush, they crawled together out the far side.

The herd stood before them.

Philip chambered a round in his hunting rifle and handed it to Hemingway. Hemingway set up for the shot, then stopped.

"Philip, look."

A pride of lions stood on the other side of the clearing. They were in the hunt.

Hemingway set down the rifle and pulled out his notebook instead.

Breaking cover, the lions chased the fleeing Cape buffalo. A male lion pounced on a buffalo calf and pulled it to the ground. He had begun to crush its neck with his powerful jaws when, astonishingly, a group of four male Cape buffalos returned to defend their young.

The lion had hesitated a mere second too long before dragging the calf off, and in so doing had opened himself to attack. One buffalo gored him; distracted, head low from the weight of his prey, a second Cape saw an opening and stomped on his beautiful man. The lion would not release his hold even after a third Cape buffalo attacked.

Sensing the lion's vulnerability, all four buffalo attacked in a fury. Finally, the lion released his hold, and from the cloud of dust the calf emerged, running to join the herd. The males soon followed.

When the red dust settled, the magnificent lion lay dead, its rivulets of crimson accentuating the hue of the plain.

It had been a titanic battle. The weak had fallen to the strong, only to be rescued by a coalition of the brave. As it should be. As the *world* should be, Hemingway thought solemnly.

A sunset on the savanna of Tanzania is almost impossible to describe. A peace descends, sanctuary returned. Orange turns to red and then purple in the cloudless sky. Hemingway took notes awkwardly, one hand on his abdomen.

Philip noticed across the dancing flames. "Papa, do you have discomfort?"

"Just a stomachache. Nothing to worry about."

But it was not just a stomachache. By dawn he was delirious with amoebic dysentery. They waited all that day for a rescue flight. When the aircraft touched down, Hemingway and Pauline were quickly loaded and flew straight to Nairobi, Kenya.

Hemingway's experience became inspiration for his writing. Upon returning to Key West in early 1934, he excitedly began a book on their travels. He also purchased a fishing vessel and named it the Pilar. That was the beginning of his love affair with the sea and fishing.

Safari—the Maasai word for hunt—was introduced to the western world by Hemingway in his book *The Green Hills of Africa*. He put great effort into the book, wanting to share Africa with his readers. But it was not well-received, and he plunged into depression, dreaming often of the eyes of the porter. In the dreams, the warrior whispered a warning to Hemingway, but it was in the language of the Maasai.

PART II: THE YANG

CHAPTER 15

THE REVOLUSIONIST

Josef Stalin's paranoia was surpassed only by his cruelty. He saw an enemy, a spy, an anti-revolutionary in every face. Coupled with his psychopathic personality, this spelt doom not just for his enemies but for the entire citizenry of the Soviet Union.

It was Stalin who initiated the Great Purge. Blood flowed from millions of innocents. It would become one of history's most profound blood-lettings. The carnage was self-inflicted, and confined only to the Soviet. So classically Russian.

As the purge metastasized from real opposition, to perceived opposition, and finally to the general citizenry, all Soviet officers were pressed into its service. Comrade Petrovski was one of these—and one of Stalin's best. He started as a propaganda writer in the Zampolite, the political police, and was ultimately transferred to the NKVD, the Soviet secret police.

It started with the gulags. But leaving one's enemies to a slow death was deemed a potential threat. Thus the purge moved on to adopt widespread executions. It was then recognized that the children of the executed might become a threat in the future—and if you exterminated that threat, then the mothers must go too. And so the purge expanded, bit by bit. Body by body.

Old scores were settled and new ones created, through the use of the Soviet grave. And opportunism fed the beast. If a peasant coveted his neighbor's land, a mere whisper to the Soviet would have that neighbor and his family out of the way by morning.

Petrovski exploited the human weaknesses of fear, revenge, jealousy, and greed. He didn't embrace the dark side of mankind, but he reveled in the orgy of blood it unleashed.

As he watched the surviving members of a village bury the men, women, and children he had just slaughtered for crimes against the Proletariat, a leaf falling from a tree caught his attention. It settled into the pit of the dead, next to a little child's hand. The hand opened and closed, grasping for life.

A shovel of Russian earth entombed it.

This meant nothing to him. It simply was. No more, no less.

He pulled his collar up against the autumn breeze and walked to his staff car.

CHAPTER 16

THE UNDEFEATED

1935

Pilar bobbed gently in the deep water south of Bimini. A warm trade wind blew across her deck and through her cabin. Hemingway was reclined in the fighting chair, napping.

She was thirty-eight feet in length, with a twelve-foot beam and beautiful hardwood construction. But her best attribut was her shallow draft of three feet six inches. Hemingway could take her anywhere in the Caribbean and not worry about running aground. Pilar was the perfect fishing vessel to explore the area.

"Fish on!" yelled Carlos, his first mate.

Hemingway sprang to action. The reel sung. He poured salt water over the spool to keep it from overheating, then put his feet on the boat's rail. He was once again engaged in the struggle.

He fought the ocean beast for hours. His entire body throbbed—arms, legs, back. He was near exhaustion when the marlin breached.

"Magnificent! Did you see that, Carlos?"

"It's a trophy, Papa. Maybe another record fish!"

"It's a fighter, I can tell you that. It will not go gently into the night or day."

Re-energized after seeing the great sailfish, he continued to reel it in, a couple of hard fought turns at a time.

Suddenly the line went slack.

"He's running to us, Carlos! All ahead on the trolling motor."

Pilar had two separate engines and propellers: a seventy-five-horsepower Chrysler for the main propulsion and a four-horsepower Lycoming trolling motor.

Hemingway reeled furiously to get tension back on the line. But he couldn't keep up—the fish was too fast.

"Go to main propulsion! Fire up the Chrysler!"

Carlos lit off the main engine as the Lycoming screamed at full power. He quickly got the Pilar up to its max speed of sixteen knots.

"My God, Carlos, he's keeping up! He's running straight at us! Turn to port, sixty degrees."

The line went taut as Hemingway spun the reel like a madman. But only temporarily. The blue marlin would have none of it. He changed course to match the Pilar's and began to leap into the air, even higher than the Pilar's seventeen feet. Its blue and silver scales glistened in the afternoon sun.

Then it dove deep and turned away, using the line to steal speed from the Pilar.

"He's outside our radius of turn—he's actually using us like a water-skier would, to get momentum! Have you ever heard of such a thing?"

"No, Papa, never. *¡Pesca el diablo!*"

The line went slack again.

"Turn to starboard, sixty degrees!"

Carlos spun the wheel, and the Pilar heeled to port as it turned to starboard violently. Hemingway nearly came out of the fighting chair.

"Here he comes!"

A streak of iridescent color erupted from the ocean a mere thirty yards behind them. It took the form of a flipping fish fighting for its life.

"I must have you!" Hemingway shouted across the sea.

It ran again, this time away from the Pilar.

"Cut the engine, Carlos, he's running. But he's weakening—I feel it!"

Tragedy slashed at the surface—a dorsal fin. Then another and yet another circled the marlin as Hemingway pulled it close.

"No, no! The devil has come to take back his fish. Carlos, get the Thompson."

The sharks continued to circle as Hemingway pulled the marlin within ten yards. Carlos handed him the Thompson sub-machine gun. He banged the open breech weapon on the boat's rail and chambered a round.

"Be careful not to shoot yourself again, Papa."

Hemingway swung the Tommy gun over the side and with one hand let loose a fusillade of .45 caliber. Blood and bullets ran across the surface. With his other arm, he held the pole, and felt it when the line went slack.

"Dammit, no! Carlos, reel him in!"

Hemingway peppered the surface, but all the blood and bullets did was draw more sharks, and they now tore into the majestic marlin. One shark came too close to the side of the boat, and Hemingway smashed it in the head with the butt of the Thompson.

Even in the midst of a feeding frenzy of sharks, Hemingway fought for his fish. He put a new magazine in the gun and killed two more sharks before he could get the hook from the Pilar's hoist into the Marlin's gill.

The surface of the water became a boiling cauldron of fins, foam, and blood. Carlos cranked the hoist, and the great marlin's head rose, its bold body glistening. But its lower half was gone—reclaimed by the sharks.

"The devil got his share, Carlos. The devil got his share…"

Hemingway looked north across the dark blue of deep water to the turquoise of the shallows. Beyond that, he imagined, the water gently caressing the roots of the mango trees. He closed his eyes and sucked it all into his memory. Everything. He would use it someday—of that he was sure.

Turning to face the sun, he let its warmth dry the sweat on his body.

"Shall I bait another line, Papa?"

Hemingway gave Carlos a deep introspective smile and shook his head. He glanced at what was left of his fish, gently swaying from the halyard. After a moment, he patted Carlos on the shoulder and said, "No."

* * *

Taking the Helm, Hemingway motored north to Bimini. Back on the fisherman's wharf, they weighed the marlin—or what they had of it. It came in at five hundred pounds. A large gathering of onlookers formed as the upper half of the once-magnificent sailfish hung from its tail, which was all that was left of the lower half, besides the spine and sail.

"I'll be, Papa," said the judge in charge of weighing. "You are going to win this tournament with less than half a damn fish. Never have I seen such a thing. Never."

He shook his old sea curmudgeon head, pulled his tattered captain's cap to cover his weathered eyes, and limped back down the pier to the judges' stand.

Hemingway turned to Carlos and shrugged. "What a fight, eh?"

"It is so sad—this was a world record fish. A world record, I'm sure."

Hemingway grabbed him around the shoulder, and they began to walk down the pier toward his favorite bar.

"It's the fight, Carlos, the *struggle* that matters. We shall never fight a fish like that again. It is fitting that the devil himself took part in it."

This should have been the happiest of times for Hemingway, and it was. He was writing material at an impressive pace, Pauline had become the Gertrude Stein of Key West, and he had his boys with him often on adventures. But even on the deck of his beloved Pilar, wrestling great fish, he felt the pull of Europe. It lay across the ocean—smoldering, beckoning.

CHAPTER 17

WINE OF WYOMING

1936

A sun-filled valley pushed the darkness away. September had come briskly. Its air swept through the mountains of the valley, warning of winter. The warning went unheeded. Twigs snapped, branches moved, but they did not reveal what disturbed them. It circled. It probed. It hunted!

Alarmed, the hunting guide grabbed Hemingway's thick wool collar and backed them both away. His bravado was gone. He was scared. A great danger lurked; death, not winter, was in the air now.

Brown fury exploded from the wicket, and a guttural roar broke the silent air. Claws propelled an immense bear toward them at an unbelievable speed.

Stumbling backwards, the guide released Hemingway's collar and tried to pull a .44-caliber pistol from its holster. But before he could draw it, he fell back over a moss-covered log.

Silence. Total silence. The guide's screaming, the bear's grunting, the heavy paws pounding the earth… Hemingway heard none of it. Only his heartbeat pulsed a steady rhythm to his brain.

Calmly, with practiced precision, he raised his .50-caliber Hawken rifle. The bear stormed within twenty paces, then ten, its eyes red with fury.

A concussion rent the air, releasing the cacophony of sound: grunts, screams, the shot's echoes. Twelve feet of grizzly bear crashed to the ground at Hemingway's feet—shot through the left eye.

"Jesus, Papa, we should be dead! Horribly dead!"

"Do you feel it?" Hemingway said.

"What?"

"The struggle." He whispered.

Hemingway bent over to examine his trophy. "We are lucky. Lucky to be in the struggle, and worthy of life."

* * *

A fire crackled in the large stone hearth, heating the room and bathing it in a soft luminescence that only a fire could. The light danced gently over the faces of the sleepy children and the deep brown log walls. Across the floor lay a large bearskin rug, with one eye deliberately sewn shut. Hemingway looked down upon his victory, an elbow perched on the mantel, a whiskey in his other hand.

Pauline drank in the scene from the doorway. "Papa," she said, "the season is ending. Shall we go back to Key West?"

He turned his attention to his drink, swirling it in contemplation. His thick leather hunting boots were crossed at the toes, and his red plaid, wool hunting shirt glowed from the fire behind him. She loved him—in spite of him, because of him. He was a man. Doubt never entered his mind; confidence permeated his soul. He moved forward, never back.

He was dangerous, not to her or the children, but to the world. Women sensed it, coveted it. She had watched, so many times, as they tried. Just as she had.

"Put the children to bed," he said.

When she came back the next time, the children all tucked away, she wore a silk gown he had bought for her in Paris. He stood in front of the fire, now bare-chested, holding out a glass of champagne. Flickering light made the effervescent liquid sparkle like distant stars in the vibrant Idaho sky.

She took the offered flute, and he took her in his arms. They made love on the bearskin rug while the fire crackled and the owls called into the darkness.

After, they stretched out on the rug in the warmth of the fire's embrace. He re-filled their glasses. She took a sip and lit a cigarette.

"Seriously, Papa, what now?"

"I have to get to Spain."

"But you are a successful novelist now. You don't need to do war correspondence anymore."

"I have to write *genuine*, Pauline. You know that."

"It's so dangerous."

"Life is dangerous. Ask the bear."

For her, it was dangerous in other ways. In his personal struggles during war, he had always reached out for the comfort of a woman. She feared Spain would be no different.

"Papa, why must you hurt those who help you, even the ones you love?"

"A man sometimes must be an island, Pauline. To prove he can stand on his own in life." He paused. "Or maybe I just hurt them before they hurt me."

CHAPTER 18

THE BUTTERFLY AND THE TANK

1937

Barcelona had been dragged into the darkness of war. Worse, it was civil war. Spaniard against Spaniard. Hemingway was there, ostensibly to cover the war as a correspondent, but in reality to lead a company of the Lincoln Brigade against the fascist forces in combat.

When Germany entered the war on the fascist side, the scale didn't just tip, it fell right off the table. Stuka dive-bombers became the Grim Reaper of the Republican troops. It tore them to shreds and hunted them relentlessly. Covered by the powerful Messerschmitt 109, the fascists owned the sky.

Hemingway watched as a Me-109 slashed at a pathetically outmatched Soviet Polikarpov I-15. Aviation had advanced at breakneck pace in the 1930s, led by German scientists. And the 109 was a technological marvel—aerodynamically sleek, with a powerful Daimler-Benz 605A-1 engine. The 109 toyed with the old Soviet biplane like a cruel cat with a wounded mouse.

A second Me-109 joined the pummeling. It dawned on Hemingway, as he watched from thousands of feet below, that this was a training exercise. A very serious training exercise. One man practicing killing another man in an air machine. Luftwaffe pilots were not just fighting a Spanish civil war—they were preparing for the next World War.

The teacher put a long burst of twenty-millimeter cannon into the I-15 to put it out of its misery. As it began to burn, the pilot bailed out. Curiously, he didn't open his parachute right away. Instead he free fell quite some distance before it finally blossomed.

The reason why became apparent when the German swooped down and lined up on the helpless pilot, hanging in his chute, floating slowly toward the ground in the still Iberian air. In defiance, the pilot pulled out a pistol and shot at the 109 just before its cannon erupted, killing him.

The pupil fired his guns toward the lifeless body, exercise complete, the two ME-109s sped away.

Hemingway watched the pilot's dead body crumple into the field. He'd had an epiphany as he witnessed the futility of that final engagement. It was a microcosm of the war.

"On your feet," he said. "The Stukas will come now. *Vamanos*."

Hemingway's sergeant pointed to the dead pilot, shrouded in his own parachute. "What about him?"

Hemingway shook his head. "Leave him. He is gone. It is the way of the Maasai."

His sergeant stared at him, confused, perhaps thinking it was a translation issue. Hemingway did not explain further.

There is no worse war than a civil war: all battles are on sovereign soil, all casualties are your own, all collateral damage is borne by the country and its people. Spain was no different, maybe worse. A gentle, congenial people had been turned rabid by the hounds of war. They tore at each other with a ferocity that was not of this world.

And in the midst of it all, Hemingway felt himself plunging again into the abyss. Not surprisingly, he sought refuge in the same place he always had—in the same place Pauline had known he would. This time, her name was Martha Gellhorn.

Ernest and Pauline's marriage would end much like the war would: with a whimper, not a bang.

CHAPTER 19

THE GARDEN OF EDEN

1939

Gregorio Fuentes docked the Pilar at the Havana City Pier. He had been Hemingway's first mate ever since a scorned lover had stolen Carlos for her boat upon learning of Hemingway's affair with Martha Gellhorn. Pauline and Hemingway had separated, too, and he was now looking for both a new home and a place to hide.

Much like Paris was Hadley, Key West was Pauline.

He was running away. Like all the relationships in his life— Hadley, Gertrude, F. Scott Fitzgerald, even his original mentor Sherwood Anderson—his relationship with Pauline had flourished, floundered, and then run aground. Because of him.

And each time he ran. Why? He didn't know.

Lively music and heavenly scents filled the air. He slapped Gregorio on the back and then left strutting down the quay as if he knew exactly where he was going.

Gregorio found him some hours later, sitting at a ridiculously small sidewalk table at a small café called El Foritinda.

Hemingway practically flung a chair at his first mate. "Sit," he demanded with a wink as he pushed a fresh whiskey to him.

"Pilar is moored and the fuel tanks are topped off. What now, Papa?"

"What now…? I suppose we await our next adventure, another war."

"What?"

"Never mind. The casinos here are nice and have beautiful women. We can start there. After a few more cocktails, of course."

After more than a few more cocktails and a feast of skirt steak, fried plantains, and red beans and rice, the two men walked to a quaint establishment in old Havana called the Hotel Ambos Mundos. Hemingway booked a room on the fifth floor with a view of the bay and the Pilar.

*　*　*

When Martha Gellhorn joined them in Havana, she immediately began a search for a winter home, one that would be permanent. Eventually she found Finca Vigia, Lookout Farm, fifteen miles outside of Havana. It was beautiful, exactly what she wanted—and she knew Hemingway would love it. Built in 1886 by a Catalan architect, the single-story hacienda had an open floor plan with two studies and a library. Its veranda overlooked the small village of San Francisco de Paula, with Havana visible in the distance. The ten-acre grounds held a guest house, a pool, and a tennis court. It was an incredibly beautiful and tranquil retreat.

Hemingway threw down the copy of the *Havana Times* and shook his head in disbelief.

"Peace in our time. Idiot! Chamberlain is an absolute idiot."

"Papa," said Martha, "why don't you work on your next novel instead?"

He grunted, walked over to the bar, mixed a gin and tonic, and stepped out onto the veranda. As he sipped his drink, he looked down on the peaceful valley. He felt truly contented for the first time in many years. Maybe ever. But he knew it wouldn't last. War was on the horizon in Europe. China was already ablaze.

Martha joined him. "Have you named it?"

He nodded. "*For Whom the Bell Tolls.*"

"That sounds rather ominous. Dark, even."

"We are about to enter a very dark time, Martha. Maybe the darkest in the history of the world."

CHAPTER 20

THE TORRENTS OF SPRING

1940

On May 10, 1940, Germany invaded Belgium and the Netherlands. Three Nazi Panzer corps drove to the English Channel in a classic pincer attack. Encircled at Dunkirk, the British Expeditionary Force and much of the French Army dug in.

Churchill ordered they be evacuated on May 22, rather than make a symbolic last stand or attempt a breakout. The Sixty-Eighth Infantry Division and the Second Light Mechanical Division of the French Army engaged the Germans to hold them off as long as possible.

By the fourth of June, the British Expeditionary Force and a large portion of the French Army had evacuated. Ten days later, Nazi tanks rolled through the Arc de Triomphe in Paris as Frenchmen wept and women sobbed. The City of Light went dark.

Colonel Schrict of the SS strutted into the file room of the Prefecture de Police, Paris. He demanded all the files be opened and got his administration team to begin constructing a list of names and addresses of known criminals, homosexuals, Gypsies, and Jews.

Schrict had moved up from propagandist, to beer hall storm trooper, to a man who dealt effectively with unpleasantries. Specifically, the purging from society of the unwanted. Unwanted by Nazi standards, of course. A purification of race was how he preferred to think of it. He had become so effective at this job that Himmler himself had ordered him to France to begin the protocol immediately.

While his men tore through files, he sat on a desk, one leg on the floor stretched straight, the other dangling. His black hat was at a rakish tilt, and the sunlight flooding in from the large windows glinted off the skull-and-crossbones emblem. A jackboot, highly polished, swung back and forth in boredom. He tapped his crop on the black pantaloons of his uniform while absently tugging at the matching tunic's collar.

His gaze wandered to the corner, where a dust-covered alligator suitcase sat, partially hidden behind a file cabinet. He rose, retrieved it, and placed it on the desk, before making a futile attempt at dusting it off with his riding crop. He glanced at the evidence tag, but it meant nothing to him; he didn't read French. He unlatched it and shuffled through the contents. His eyes went wide with recognition.

"Herr Colonel, shall I process the contents?" asked an aide.

"*Nein*, Herr Hauptman. I shall see to this personally. Have it taken to my room at the Ritz. Seal it, my eyes only."

"*Jawohl*, Herr Colonel." The man clicked his heels and exited the room with the suitcase.

Unable to suppress a smile, Schrict decided some French wine and lunch were in order. His men were well-trained; they didn't need his oversight. "Carry on," he ordered as he marched from the room.

*   *   *

Weeks turned to months as Schrict painstakingly translated each manuscript. Magnificent stories revealed themselves one page at a time. Like an archeologist, he took his time. But he was not just translating; he was modifying. Carefully he changed the locations to German cities and towns. He made the heroes Nazis, the villains British. No doubt these manuscripts would please the party and make him quite rich after the war.

He knew American literature—he had studied it before failing out of university—so he knew these had not been published. The carbons further verified that. These were the only copies. And by the dates, he knew they had been written in Paris. How appropriate.

His French concubine spoke German, so he read passages of the stories to her. She was quite impressed, and gave him her favor easily and voraciously.

Yes, he would make them his own.

CHAPTER 21

ONE TRIP ACROSS

1941

Martha's magazine assigned her to China to do a series on the war. Japan had invaded like locusts, and unbridled barbarity swept through the ancient nation. It was as if the Mongols had swept down from the plains again, and this time the Great Wall would not hold them back.

Hemingway watched the marbled blue and turquoise water dance beneath the train. Colors swirled and changed with the depth of the water: channels blue, sandbars turquoise, the reef blue-brown. He already missed Pilar.

It was his favorite part of the trip each time he left Key West. A single rail line serpentined up the Keys, much of it raised like the L in Chicago, only higher. It provided an excellent view, making him feel as though he were on a long, slow, low-flying aircraft.

He and Martha had stopped in at Key West to see the children before going overseas. It had been awkward, to say the least. Key West was no longer his.

He studied their itinerary as they continued toward Miami. A Pan Am Clipper would fly them to Los Angeles, change crews and refuel, then continue to Hawaii. They'd overnight there before flying to Midway Island, then Wake, and ultimately landing in Manila Bay, Philippines. After a rest in Manila they'd continue on to China.

As he stepped from the cab, Hemingway glanced down the dock of Pan Am's seaplane aerodrome on Dinner Island in Biscayne Bay. An immense Boeing 314 flying boat was tied to the end. Mechanics swarmed all over the machine doing final checks before its planned months-long journey around the world. It was a risky ambition; with a significant portion of the world at war, the route became more in question every day. More in doubt. Fascism was sweeping the planet. Europe and the Orient were already being overrun. And it would only get worse. Much worse.

Hemingway felt helpless to stop it. Spain had been a futile attempt. "A noble effort" they called it, but of course *they* had not been there. Noble it was not. Wanton slaughter was not noble. Of course, he had contributed to the perception with his latest novel.

For Whom the Bell Tolls continued to do quite well and had propelled him back to the top of American writers. It had also allowed him to buy Finca Vigia. He loved it there, basking in the sun. But the same dark forces as always had pulled him back to war. He just had to find a way to get into it. Being a tourist at arm's length would not do.

"Papa, what are you scheming?" said Martha.

"Huh? What, my dear?"

"Don't give me that huh, what. I see it in your eyes."

"I don't know what you could possibly mean."

She gave him a look of warning as they stepped onto the magnificent aircraft. The Atlantic Clipper truly was luxurious, and they were traveling first class. It had been pulled off the northern European route and was now flying the Pacific.

Spotting an army major making his way toward coach—and noting the Signal Corps insignia on the lapel of the officer's khaki uniform jacket—Hemingway grabbed two champagnes from an offered silver platter and headed straight for the man.

"Major, a cocktail?"

The man turned. He quite obviously recognized Hemingway, but did not react outwardly. "I'm afraid I'm in the cheap seats, Mr. Hemingway."

"Nonsense. We are moving you up. Follow me."

They rejoined Martha and found a steward.

"Steward," said Hemingway, "can you accommodate Major...?"

"Anderson, sir."

"Yes, Major Anderson, with us in first class? On our tab, of course."

Martha looked sideways at him.

He whispered into her ear. "He's in the Signal Corps, intelligence I'd bet. We can find out what's really going on. Besides, you can expense it."

He winked at her, and she smiled in spite of herself.

Soon all three were seated at a small table with a tray of hors d'oeuvres. Hemingway detailed their journey to China for Martha's magazine and asked Major Anderson where he was going.

"Manila," the man answered.

"Manila? What command is that?"

Anderson hesitated, and then spoke generically about a staff position.

"Intelligence, eh, major?"

"I didn't say that, Mr. Hemingway."

"You didn't have to. Call me Papa."

Anderson looked long and hard at Hemingway, as though trying to figure out if he was the man he was rumored to be, or just another celebrity.

All fourteen cylinders of a Twin Wasp popped and then finally fired evenly, allowing a steady idle. Each of the four Wright GR-2600 engines rumbled to life separately. Once all four were humming smoothly, Hemingway turned once more to Anderson.

"Send a cable to DC when we get to Los Angeles and ask them if they want an agent in China. This will be my fourth war, Major."

Anderson glanced at Martha, who shrugged in response as if already bored by the subject. Turning back to Hemingway, he nodded once. Then he offered his hand.

"Call me Frank."

Conversation then turned to fishing and hunting. Anderson had hunted often as a boy, and the two men shared hunting stories that drove Martha to her book.

Dinner was a splendid trout almandine, with scalloped potatoes and French-cut green beans that were fried in a delicate butter and garlic sauce. The French wine was exquisite, and they savored it, knowing that soon it would not be available.

After waving off desert, Anderson excused himself from the table. Martha watched as he went through a hatch toward the crew area.

"Where is he going?" she asked.

"I suppose to the radio shack."

She looked at him. "You aren't serious about this, are you?"

Hemingway shrugged. "It will give me something to do while you work."

*   *   *

Anderson handed the radioman a message he had written out from a small book. The man looked at the seemingly nonsensical letters, raised an eyebrow, then turned to the telegraph and sent the message.

Anderson tapped a cigarette out of a pack of Lucky Stripes, and offered one to the radioman as well. He struck his Zippo and lit both. Neither man spoke.

Thirty-five minutes later, a coded response was received. Anderson smiled, thanked the radioman, and headed aft. He found Hemingway relaxing with a gin and tonic.

"So, this isn't your first rodeo."

Hemingway smiled and motioned toward an empty seat.

"I passed along some information Major, especially on the tactics and effectiveness of the Luftwaffe in Spain. Apparently it was well received."

He waved over a steward and ordered fresh cocktails for them both. He didn't speak again until the steward had set down the cocktails and left.

"How can I help you, Frank?" Hemingway asked.

Anderson put an attaché case on the table, unlocked it, and snapped it open. He pulled out a map of China and laid it on the table, using the open case to hide it from view.

"China is a tough nut to crack," he said. "A thousand years' worth of intrigue, and it's really been a mess since the fall of the last dynasty.

To be honest, Papa, we don't know what is going on. We've been dumping weapons into China by the shipload, but we don't see any results. Hell, we think the Japanese might have fought the Russians on the China border in '39. But now it's quiet."

"A truce?"

Anderson looked around, then shrugged. "We don't know. But if they do have one, that has huge strategic implications."

He gathered up the map and returned it to the attaché case. Then he motioned for Hemingway to follow him. The two men walked into the crew area, stopping at the communication compartment.

"Could we borrow your area for a bit?" Anderson asked.

The radioman looked at them both, then at his watch. "I just made a position report, so sure, it will be a couple hours until I need to make another."

After the radioman left, Anderson pulled the narrow door closed behind them, and he and Hemingway crowded around the small table. Opening his case once more, Anderson spread documents out on the table.

"We don't have much. What I do know is that Mao Zedong and the Nationalists are not playing well together."

"What are the Communists up to?"

"Not sure. Mao seems to have solidified power among the movement. Lots of comrades suddenly disappeared."

"Are you sure it's Mao and not the Japanese?"

"Zhou Enlai?"

"Enlai has apparently teamed up with Mao."

Hemingway nodded and lit two cigarettes, passing one to Anderson. Smoke filled the tiny space. He could tell Anderson was hesitant to continue.

After taking a deep drag, Anderson exhaled slowly, making up his mind.

"Do you believe in intuition Papa?"

"Absolutely."

"I think Mao is making a play for all of China. He is gambling that the Allies will win the war."

"Damn big gamble, Frank."

"Is it?"

"You tell me. I'm just a writer."

Anderson gave Hemingway a knowing smile. "I don't think it is, Papa. Why did Germany lose the first world war?"

"Too many fronts. Tactics. Supply shortages... the truce!"

"Yes. If Japan and Russia have a secret armistice, then the Soviets can withdraw and wait for winter—and move the divisions on the Mongolian and Chinese borders to the Eastern Front. Zhou Enlai is the diplomat, Mao the warrior; together they put together a truce with the Nationalists to fight the Japanese. When we defeat the Axis..."

"If," quipped Hemingway.

Anderson nodded. "*If* we defeat the Axis, Mao will use our weapons, which he has been stockpiling, to destroy the Nationalist Army and seize all of China."

Hemingway looked at the map, studying the battle lines and occupied areas. Hitler already had all of Eastern Europe. "You think Hitler is dumb enough?"

"If he thinks the Imperial Japanese Army will cross into Russia in support, yes, I do."

"And if Japan doesn't, then what?"

"Look at that scale, Papa. Imagine trying to supply troops even a third of the way into Russia."

"Winter."

Anderson nodded in agreement. "Napoleon won at Borodino…"

"But the winter defeated him. Wellington knew it and waited for him at Waterloo," Hemingway finished. "And what do the Russians think?"

"FDR has tried to warn them of an imminent invasion, but they think we're just trying to drag them into the war. Remember they have a treaty with Hitler."

"Yeah, they split the Balkans between them. What do you want from me?"

"I'll be honest with you: most everyone else thinks I'm nuts. I do have the ear of the United States Treasury Secretary, Henry Morganthau. He'll listen, but he wants some hard intel. I need to know where the weapons we're shipping are actually going, and what kind of shape the Nationalists are in. But most of all, I need to know if there's a truce between Russia and Japan."

"So, everything?"

Anderson laughed. "Yep."

"Why Treasury?"

"I suspect he's concerned with another Communist nation rising out of the ashes of China. Hardly good for capitalism and the US Treasury. It also means Japan won't have to worry about its northern flank with Russia when they fight us in the Pacific."

Hemingway shook his head. "Soviets! The duplicitous bastards."

"Papa, the Communists are in it for the long haul, all of them. They have nothing, so they have nothing to lose."

CHAPTER 22

A MAN OF THE WORLD

February 22, 1941

Penetrating through the winter overcast, the China Clipper banked just over a Chinese junk, lined up on a clear area, and settled onto the dark waters of Victoria Bay. Engines snorted to a stop as it drifted onto the tug's cart. Ground crew quickly secured the flying boat, and the tug's diesel engine strained and smoked under the load as it pulled the Boeing from the water.

Journalists, long anticipating Hemingway's arrival, crowded around the clipper's stairs as they were put in place. He emerged first, of course, then waved for Martha to join him on the platform. She tried not to roll her eyes as she waved to his subjects.

"They love us already, Martha," he whispered into her ear.

"It is you they love, Papa. Me they don't even notice."

"Nonsense, Martha, they—"

He stopped mid-sentence, his jaw sagging as he looked beyond the crowd and saw a perfect white braid moving away from him. He strained to see a face.

"Papa? Papa! What is it? Are you sick? Papa?"

"No—I'm—I'm fine. Let's get to the hotel."

He waved off her questions and smiled as they descended the stairs.

A young British captain stepped into their path as they walked toward the Star Ferry terminal. "Mr. Hemingway." He snapped off a sharp salute. "Captain Charles Boxer. Major Anderson thought I might be of assistance."

*   *   *

They moved together silently onto the crowded Star Ferry. It quickly got underway from the Kowloon pier toward the Hong Kong side of the bay. "Bustling" was the only word to describe the city of Hong Kong. Even at war, the trading mecca throbbed with activity. As they disembarked, Boxer waved them toward a waiting Rolls Royce. The hotel's name was written on the side: The Hong Kong Hotel.

"Thank you, Captain," said Martha, "but we are staying at the Repulse Bay Hotel."

"Mrs. Hemingway, I've taken the liberty of putting you in the honeymoon suite of the Hong Kong."

"Really?" she replied with irritation.

Boxer directed his response to Hemingway. "The major thought it would be ideal."

As they got in the limo, Martha sat back, not pleased with the change of itinerary. She could see that her assignment for *Collier's*

Weekly magazine was quickly becoming a sideshow for another of Ernest Hemingway's adventures. Crossing her arms tightly, she looked out the window in disgust.

Hemingway leaned forward, waiting for her to make eye contact. When she glanced his way, he gave her a broad smile and a wink. She couldn't help herself—she grinned in return. Then, angry at her lack of self-control, she turned to the window again.

"As I was saying, sir…"

"Call me Papa, Charles."

"I don't think that is appropriate under the circumstances."

"Nonsense. Papa is the name my friends call me. If we are to be friends then you must do so as well."

"As you wish, sir."

Hemingway raised a brow and held it.

"Papa."

"Excellent. What have you for us, Captain?"

"Well, sir—er, Papa. We have arranged a small party with some individuals that shall become your…"

"Entourage," Martha snapped.

Captain Boxer cleared his throat nervously. "Yes, quite. We should like it to appear you are merely…"

"Getting drunk with his entourage."

"Indeed."

"Won't that be nice," muttered Martha. "And I'm to play the hostess to this entourage of… of desperadoes, no doubt."

"Yes, ma'am, we'd rather hoped—"

"Well forget it. I'm a journalist on assignment. You boys have fun playing spy."

"Now, Martha," Hemingway began.

"Don't 'now Martha' me, Ernest. This isn't our first rodeo, and I don't intend to be the clown while you ride the bull."

She turned once more to the refuge of the window and watched as the city shifted from ancient to modern.

* * *

Hemingway bypassed the front desk and went directly to the lobby bar, The Grips. Boxer introduced him to some diplomats, a few pilots from the Chinese National Aviation Company (CNAC), and the legendary—or notorious, depending on one's point of view—Morris "Two-Gun" Cohen, a cockney character of Polish-Jewish heritage. He had somehow risen to the rank of general in the Kuomintang.

Hemingway pumped hands and slapped backs as he worked the room. Reporters from the Hong Kong papers shouted questions and greetings.

Charles steered Hemingway to a table with Two-Gun and a crew of CNAC pilots.

"Gentlemen, may I introduce Ernest Hemingway."

"Call me Papa," Hemingway said. "What are we drinking, gents?"

"A bit early, isn't it, sir?"

"Nonsense, not with the proper cocktail."

Hemingway waved over a waiter. "My good man. Get a large beer pitcher, fill it with ice, a bottle of tomato juice, one liter of vodka, an equal dash of black and cayenne pepper, and shake in just a bit of celery salt. Add a tablespoon, no more no less, of Worcestershire sauce. A full jigger of fresh-squeezed lime juice, and then bring it to me with two fingers of vodka in a tumbler."

The waiter took copious notes, then hurried back to the bar and handed the recipe to the bartender. The bartender looked up to see Hemingway giving him a thumbs-up and a wink.

After meticulously following the directions, the bartender sampled the concoction, smiled to himself, and delivered the cocktail to Hemingway's table personally.

"Mr. Hemingway—"

"Papa. I know we are going to be friends."

"As you wish, sir. Papa, does this delightful pick-me-up have a name?"

Hemingway turned to his captive audience and beamed. "Bloody Mary."

"How wonderfully sacrilegious," the bartender replied, with just a hint of sarcasm. "Might I steal your formula?"

"I'll trade it for your *nom de guerre*."

"Archibald, at your service." The man bowed deeply, with sincerity.

"It's all yours, Archie. Use it in good health."

Hemingway sampled his masterpiece as if he were tasting the finest French wine. "Hm. It lacks authority."

He dumped the tumbler of vodka into the pitcher and stirred it with a pen from his pocket. Tapping the pen on the pitcher's edge, he then wiped it clean with his lips, taking a second sample. He declared it perfect.

"Shall I pour, Papa?" asked one of the pilots.

Across the lobby, out the glass doors, Hemingway spotted a white braid. It was distorted by the prism of beveled glass and snapped in and out of focus.

"Shall I pour?"

"Huh?" he said. "Ah, yes. By all means pour, good sir."

* * *

After settling in to the hotel room, Martha walked down to the hotel bar, where she found the king and his court. They were already animated and obviously on their way to being drunk. She shook her head with a smile—again in spite of herself—and left them to their business, easing out the ornate doors and into the street.

Leaving the main thoroughfare, Martha stepped down a dark alley that was more of a time portal than a simple paved path. Steep walls jutted into the darkening sky, looming over the transitioning scene. Below, lean-tos and their contents provided dingy and faded color to the otherwise drab scene. In the nearest shelter, an open flame licked at an old wok, in which sesame oil crackled, bathing vegetables and a bit of unrecognizable meat. An ancient woman huddled over the meal, breathing in its fragrance.

Farther along, another old woman wept openly, clutching a dead cat to her breast. As Martha tried to pass, the woman wailed, held the cat up, and nodded out the alley toward the busy street.

Martha followed her nod. A Rolls Royce flashed abruptly past the opening, like a rip in time.

Shrieking in Cantonese, the aggrieved woman thrust the dead feline at Martha again, demanding acknowledgment of the atrocity.

Unsure what else to do, Martha awkwardly reached out and petted the cat, saying she was sorry. Then she stepped over a passed-out opium addict and slipped away.

In every alleyway and side street the scene was repeated in various ways. It felt to Martha like these makeshift villages could be a thousand years old. Hong Kong was a veneer, she thought. A false front. Was all of China like this?

This was the story she wanted to tell.

* * *

Hemingway awoke, squinting through bloodshot eyes, to find Martha handing him a cup of coffee balanced on a matching saucer. Steam rose from it, promising slight respite from the fog that hung over him.

"It's all bullshit," she said.

He wiped his hand over his face and sat up. "What, exactly, is bullshit, my dear?"

"China."

"China? The entire country?"

She nodded confidently as she sipped her own coffee. "Nothing is real; it's like a Hollywood set. Once you leave the main boulevards you see the real China. Poverty. Prostitution. Opium. Desperation. They are showing us bullshit, Papa."

Hemingway nodded in agreement. He had suspected the same of the Nationalist Army and the government itself. In his short time here, as a veteran of two wars, it had been clear to him that something was amiss. He had watched the ships crammed full of war supplies disgorging at the piers of Kow Loon—and yet when they visited Chinese units, all he saw were old surplus weapons from World War One. Where were the weapons going?

"We need to take a secret tour," he said.

"How, Papa?"

"Captain Sean LaPlante of the Chinese National Aviation Company."

*   *   *

At five o'clock sharp, Hemingway swept into the bar with Martha on his arm. After glad-handing with reporters and his entourage, he slumped into a chair at a table inhabited only by Captain Sean LaPlante.

LaPlante was a gregarious thirty-year-old native of Minnesota, and he and Papa had become quick pals. Both were avid outdoorsmen. They had even hunted and fished the same areas of the northern Midwest. LaPlante also had a PhD in street smarts and intuition. He had survived, flourished even, in a war zone. His life goal was retirement, by the age of forty, to a log home in the Boundary Waters region of Minnesota.

He looked from Hemingway to Martha, who stood behind her husband, and back again. "So what do you want, Papa?"

"A tour."

"Of?"

"China. Specifically, an airfield at the front."

"Really, that's all?"

CHAPTER 23

THE STRANGE COUNTRY

March 12, 1941

Wright R-1820 cyclone engines howled at the rising sun as LaPlante shoved the throttles forward. The Hamilton Standard propellers dug into the morning air, pulling the DC-3 down the runway. Rotating into the calm air, LaPlante turned the airliner over Hong Kong Harbor and began a climbing turn toward the front. Once at cruising altitude, he turned the aircraft over to his co-pilot.

"Okay. What are you really up to, Papa?"

Hemingway was seated between LaPlante and his co-pilot, wearing the uniform of a navigator. He nodded toward the co-pilot.

LaPlante took control again and sent the co-pilot to the back.

When he was out of earshot, Hemingway smiled at LaPlante and said, calmly, "I'm a spy."

LaPlante laughed heartily. "For who?"

"For whom."

"Okay, Papa. I guess I shouldn't be surprised."

*　*　*

After bouncing to a stop on the rutted dirt runway, LaPlante throttled his way to a muddy tarmac and shut the engines down. Coolies rushed the aircraft and began to offload the cargo.

At the other end of the human conveyor belt was a line of new GMC military trucks, provided by the US of A. Hemingway walked up to the third one in line. Glancing around to make sure no one was watching, he reached into his navigation kit bag and pulled out a quart of red paint. He popped the top off with a can opener, tossed the opened container onto the green canvas top of the truck, then glanced around once more before walking back toward the aircraft.

A white braid bobbed past Hemingway. Instinctively, he thrust an arm out and grabbed the figure by the shoulder.

An old Chinaman spun to face him. Confused, he bowed to Hemingway, who apologized quickly. The man hurried off.

"What was that all about?" LaPlante asked.

"Nothing. I'll wait in the cockpit."

Three hours later they were flying toward the front, over a column of trucks snaking its way through the hills. Hemingway was now in the co-pilot seat, having displaced the second in command. He occasionally glanced down at the chart in his lap, which he was marking with the road's route. At other times he counted the trucks and looked for a red paint splat.

"How many are gone, Papa?" LaPlante asked.

"Two thirds of them."

LaPlante turned away from the front. After another forty minutes of flight he rolled up on a wing and pointed to a red-spattered truck.

"Is that what you're looking for?" he asked.

Hemingway looked over at him. "How long have you known?"

"It ain't brain surgery, Papa."

"Where are they headed?"

"Inland, to the Communist stronghold, is my bet. A better question is why?"

Hemingway marked the chart. "To fight the next war."

LaPlante looked over at Hemingway, then banked the DC-3 back on course for Hong Kong. "Okay, Papa. We'll give them a couple days and then go check."

* * *

They swept into The Grips like a blast from a Hartzell propeller. Still in a CNAC uniform, Hemingway led the charge for the bar.

"Archie, my good man. Fresh horses and whiskey for my men!"

As the shots of whiskey were set in front of the men, Morris "Two-Gun" Cohen strutted up.

"Nice suit, Papa. So you've been joyriding around China?"

"A bit, Two-Gun."

Hemingway downed a shot, grabbed an offered beer, and motioned to a quiet table. Two-Gun followed after snatching LaPlante's beer on its way to LaPlante's mouth.

"Thanks, Sean," he said with a wink.

When they were settled at the table, Two-Gun said, "So what's up, Papa?"

"You tell me, Generalissimo."

Two-Gun looked at him with a raised brow.

"A little bird told me about your commission as a general in the Kuomintang," Hemingway said. "That's The Nationalist Chinese party, correct?"

Two-Gun shrugged off the question. "And?"

"And I need a closer look at the front."

"For your magazine?"

"Of course. PM is paying me to report on the war."

Captain Boxer entered The Grips at that moment, and Hemingway raised a finger to him as if casually placing a bid. Boxer sat down with the two men. Hemingway pulled a sealed envelope from his pocket and slid it across the table.

"Here is that article I plan to submit," He said. "Could you check it for accuracy, Charles?"

* * *

March 12, 1941

Dear Frank,

I checked on some of your packages. Your suspicions are confirmed. Many are going to the wrong address. I think they may be re-routing to your Chinese gambler.

Papa

CHAPTER 24

A SIMPLE ENQUIRY

April 1, 1941

Emaciated horses and child soldiers slogged slowly through thick mud in Guangdong Province. Martha called them orphan ghosts. They weren't equipped properly. The children didn't even have shoes.

Ernest and Martha had been in the province for a week, searching for the war. Thus far they had found nothing but orphan ghosts and mud. They were miserable—war correspondents without a war. All was quiet on the Canton Front.

After a couple more days of deprivation, they journeyed to Chungking. Two-Gun Cohen had gotten them an audience with Generalissimo Chiang Kai-shek, leader of the Nationalist Party, and his wife. It did not go well. Martha challenged Madame Chiang on the feudalist system in China, insulting her. The woman snapped back that China had had a great civilization while Martha's ancestors were still living in trees.

Now Hemingway, Two-Gun, and Martha sat in a hotel bar discussing the trip and China in general.

"I'm telling you, China is a time bomb," Martha insisted.

"More than you know," Two-Gun mumbled.

"What does that mean?" Hemingway asked.

Two-Gun remained silent.

"Let's put our cards on the table, Two-Gun. What is really going on?"

"Do you really want to know?"

"Yes, we do," Martha answered.

Two-Gun sighed. "You have characterized China quite well, Martha. Feudal, lords and slaves, corrupt. Have and have not. Who do you think will win when the bomb times out?"

Two-Gun's insight was anything but self-serving. In fact, it predicted the demise of his position.

"And what will you do?" Hemingway asked.

"Move on." Two-Gun slipped into himself, then suddenly stood. "Come with me."

He led them to a market whose sights and smells thrust the yin and yang of China on their senses. Spices were juxtaposed with fish and open sewers; colored silks were but a row away from ugly, butchered meat. It was a microcosm of China.

A white braid floated through the market in and out of view. Hemingway shoved his trembling hand in his trousers pocket to hide it.

"Wait here," Two-Gun said, and disappeared into the crowd.

Twenty minutes later a slight Chinaman in a Western business suit appeared at their side. He bowed almost imperceptibly and whispered, "Would you like to meet Zhou Enlai?"

Hemingway nodded, and the young man turned and walked into the crowd.

As they followed, Ernest explained to Martha, "Zhou is the number two man in the Communist Party. A diplomat."

*   *   *

Zhou gave them a hearty welcome and invited them to tea. He was charming and knowledgeable, and together they spoke of the world and literature, as fellow intellectuals.

Finally, Hemingway asked, "Why did you ask for this meeting, Zhou?"

"Mr. Hemingway, you have seen China. You must know that the present situation is untenable."

"The Japanese?"

Zhou dismissed the question with a smile. "If a new China is to emerge in the world, it would help us to have a sympathetic voice."

"For a united China, the Kuomintang, and the Communist Party?"

Again, the man smiled away the question. "The situation is untenable."

"We aren't talking about Japan, are we?" Martha asked.

"There will be blood," said Hemingway. "We have seen a civil war up close."

"There already has been much blood, Mr. Hemingway, and there will be more. Unfortunately, that is inevitable. Those few with much will not go quietly into the night."

"Is that why you are stockpiling the weapons we ship you?"

Zhou's hand froze momentarily as he moved to drop a cube of sugar in his tea. He stirred slowly, intently, making eye contact with Hemingway. "We are on the long march," he said.

"But still Japan is in your country, killing your people."

"You have just come from the front," said Zhou. "What was your impression?"

"It's stable."

"Yes, Mr. Hemingway. Quite stable."

"Still, there are the Russians. China will be crushed between the opposing forces of Japan and Russia." Hemingway was baiting the man.

"Will we? Our Communist brothers have assured us this will not happen."

"A non-aggression pact?"

"I have said too much."

*   *   *

Back at the hotel, they found a drunk Two-Gun Cohen at the bar. He waved them to a seat.

"So how was your meeting?" he slurred.

"Interesting. The Communists seem unconcerned with the Japanese."

He nodded and laughed, a defeatist air about him. "The Imperial Japanese Army is a skin disease. The Communists are China's heart disease." After a long silence he added, "And the patient only has five to ten years to live."

CHAPTER 25

THE FIFTH COLUMN

Hemingway returned to Finca Vigia alone. He had stopped in Manila, where Frank had warned him his report would not be well received, and emphasized that Hemingway stress he was merely the messenger. So he spent weeks preparing his intelligence report before traveling to Washington, DC.

Secretary Morgenthau received him warmly, and a meeting was set up with various intelligence services, including the FBI. Hemingway presented his report. He gave a comprehensive description of the arms diversion and the weakness of the Nationalist Party as well as its army, juxtaposed against the strength of the Communists. A series of photographs verified his claims.

Silence fell over the room when he summarized the non-aggression pact between Japan and Russia. Shock registered on the assembled faces when he revealed his source. Expressions turned to anger when he shared Two-Gun Cohen's prediction.

"You spoke with Zhou Enlai? Directly?" the secretary said.

"I did. He is both charming and competent. Do not underestimate—"

"He's a goddamned *Communist*," shouted J. Edgar Hoover, the director of the FBI.

"That's the point of the report, Director. Try to keep up."

Furious, Hoover slammed his copy of the report closed. "This is garbage."

"I'm merely the messenger," Hemingway said. "Take it or leave it. But if you *do* leave it, I suggest you get your ass in the field and check for yourself."

"Gentlemen, please," said the secretary. "We are all on the same side here."

"Are we?" snapped Hoover.

Hemingway jumped to his feet so abruptly that his chair tipped back and hit the floor. "I am a private citizen—and unpaid. I do *not* have to take this abuse from a bureaucratic windbag."

Morgenthau stood as well. "Let's adjourn for today. Ernest, could you and I meet privately?"

Hoover was beet red in anger as he left the room. Hemingway lifted the chair from the floor and set it back on its legs. He, too, was still angry after the exchange.

When the room cleared, Morgenthau spoke quietly. "You have made an enemy. A very dangerous one."

"Screw him."

"Please be careful. He is quite vengeful."

"I'll send him an autographed book."

"Excellent idea. So, tell me what you think. I must admit I'm very impressed with this report. And Frank was impressed with both your analysis and your operational skills."

Hemingway nodded his thanks, as his temper cooled. "I agree with Cohen's assessment, Mr. Secretary. In fact, I don't think anything can be done. China is lost. Anything we send them will be pointed at us eventually."

Morgenthau turned in his chair and looked out the window. "How certain are you that a non-aggression pact exists between Russia and Japan?"

"Quite certain, sir."

"Why?"

"The Communists are on the long march. They will use this war to their advantage, to win the next."

"The enemy of my enemy is my friend," Morgenthau said quietly. Slowly he swiveled his chair to face Hemingway. "I agree."

"May I ask why?"

The secretary sat silently for a full minute before pulling a file from the bottom of his stack. He opened it and put his reading glasses on the tip of his nose.

"It seems Germany has mobilized on the Eastern Front to invade Russia. It is obvious even to Stalin, and he has pulled all his best divisions and command staff off the Japanese front to engage the Germans. The Japanese have not responded at all."

"Not good for us, Mr. Secretary, but worse for Germany."

"Yes, the enemy of my enemy...."

He took off his reading glasses and set them on the file. "I'm afraid we will have to leave the Chinese problem for another day."

CHAPTER 26

A PURSUIT RACE

Cuba had become his adopted home. On his hill overlooking Havana, he felt a contentment he had never experienced before.

That ended on December 7, 1941.

Japan attacked America, and war was declared. Hemingway could not sit idly by. Havana was full of Falangists—Spanish fascists—and he saw them as a threat. With the approval of the US ambassador, Spruille Braden, Hemingway set up an intelligence operation based in his guest house. His mission was to monitor the fascists.

Martha was less than impressed with the scoundrels who inhabited Finca Vigia—and did not lose sight of the fact that they drank with Papa nightly. She thought his efforts dubious at best. Hemingway poked fun at her by calling them the "crook factory."

Soon, however, Hoover found out about the crook factory. He took control of all Caribbean counterintelligence operations, leaving Hemingway out in the cold. Hemingway fumed.

However, truth be told, he had become bored with the intelligence operation. There was no action. No excitement. No danger. The real action, at least locally, was in the Caribbean, where Nazi U-boats roamed seemingly at will. They sank more shipping in the tight confines of the Caribbean than in the entire North Atlantic.

It was while Hemingway sat in his study, reading a book from his library on the exploits of British Q-boats during World War I, that he had an epiphany. The book explained that most of the Q-boats were converted fishing boats, disguised and armed to attack surfaced submarines.

"The Pilar!" he said aloud.

"What, Papa?" Martha asked.

"I can convert the Pilar to hunt Nazi subs. We can get into the fight here, and never even have to leave Cuba."

Martha rolled her eyes.

Ambassador Braden couldn't say no. The secretary of the navy had already asked East Coast yachtsmen to patrol and report submarines.

The Pilar was unable to handle heavier weapons, so it was outfitted with light machine guns, bazookas, grenades, and—for the kill—a large bomb to be dropped down a submarine's hatch. Martha repeatedly voiced concern with that portion of the plan, but Hemingway's enthusiasm wouldn't be quashed. A Marine sergeant, Don Saxon, was also attached to the Pilar, to operate the radios.

The plan was simple: they would patrol the sea lanes, looking for surfaced U-boats, and report the subs' positions to the navy. Because of the Pilar's small size, they could even search cays and small islands, looking for stashed supplies. Hemingway took the job seriously enough that he even limited his drinking while on patrol.

*   *   *

Expansive streaks of red, orange, and pink painted the blue canvas of western sky. The sun, having danced its last reflective dance of the day, slipped below the horizon leaving a red glow. Pilar's crew watched from her deck, and smiled at the good omen.

"Surely we will find one tonight," Hemingway whispered into the sunset.

He took a last longing glance before turning the Pilar toward the darkening east, and pushing up the throttle. Havana's sparkling lights faded in the Pilar's wake. Hemingway was electrified with anticipation as they motored into the night.

"Man your lookout stations," he said. "They will surface soon, to recharge their batteries."

Sergeant Saxon spread out a nautical chart on the plotting table. He had charted the planned movement of US Navy submarines out of the pens in Key West.

Hemingway looked over his shoulder from the con, and put his finger on an empty spot. "That's where I'd go, if I were a U-boat skipper."

Saxon nodded. "Let's go kill one, Papa."

Stars filled the sky as the boat bobbed on gentle swells. The twinkling lights stretched to the horizon in every direction, as if they were diamonds embedded in a gigantic inverted celestial bowl. Their brightness was staggering, illuminating the ocean surface even on this moonless night.

Pilar and the U-boats had played this cat-and-mouse game many nights, for months that now stretched into years. But so far, nothing. Darkness.

They sat, waiting. Hemingway raised his navy-issue binoculars and scanned out to where the galaxies touched the ocean.

A ripple formed in the smooth surface. A periscope. A tower. A spine. Finally, the mother sea birthed a U-boat.

"Man your battle stations, gentlemen," Hemingway whispered with confidence.

Saxon was instantly at his ear. "Should I start the engine?"

"Not yet. We will wait for him to start his."

Diesel smoke blurred and obscured the stars around the submarine.

"He's deaf now," Hemingway said. "Full speed ahead."

Pilar's engine strained at full throttle, propelling them to battle. Hemingway ordered the weapons brought up on deck from their hiding places below. Saxon handed him a Thompson submachine gun and then took position on the bow with an M1 bazooka.

* * *

At one thousand yards, a U-boat lookout heard the Pilar. He reported it to the bridge immediately.

The chief of the boat reported. "Constant bearing, decreasing range." Lowering his binoculars, he faced the U-boat's skipper in astonishment. "Is he attacking?"

A reply came in the form of a burst from Hemingway's Thompson. It rattled across the sail bridge. The two Germans faced each other, the skipper shaking his head.

"Full speed ahead, put them in our wake. Emergency dive!"

* * *

Pilar closed to five hundred yards, her crew's light machine guns barking defiance at the superior foe. The Type VII U-boat was quickly up to its top speed of eighteen knots. Pilar's Chrysler Crown

Marine engine's six cylinders were pumping out its full seventy-five horsepower, but it just wasn't enough: sixteen knots was the max speed it could generate.

"It's getting away!" Hemingway shouted above the chattering machine guns. "Fire the bazooka!"

A violent swoosh filled his ears, and a flash blinded him. But the rocket-propelled explosive fell impotently in the U-boat's wake.

"Shoot another!"

"He's out of range, Papa."

"Fire, dammit!"

His first mate launched his bazooka in a steep arc. Tracers bounced off the sail bridge. Even from here, they could hear the dive claxon.

*   *   *

The U-boat's chief slid down the ladder, followed by the skipper, who pulled the hatch closed and spun the locking mechanism. Ineffective rounds impacted the steel bridge like a jackhammer, but an explosion off the port beam rocked the sub.

*   *   *

Hanging over the bow to get closer, Hemingway jammed in another magazine and hammered away at the burble even after the U-boat was beneath the surface. Only when the Thompson was empty did he throw it down and curse the night in frustration.

*   *   *

With the U-boat in a steep dive, the skipper hung on the periscope railing and turned to his chief.

"Are they all crazy, these Americans?"

CHAPTER 27

THE DENUNCIATION

1944

Martha was done with him, and he knew it. He hadn't helped by refusing to help her get press credentials and transportation to London. *What's the point?* he thought to himself. *Just to get told off? She can do that by telegram.*

His thoughts elsewhere as he drove, he was too slow to see the face that materialized out of the dark in front of the car. *The gypsy!* Swerving hard to avoid the old woman, he struck an oncoming truck.

Hemingway was flung into the frame of the windshield.

Everything went black.

*   *   *

Her face floated through his dreams. She was in Switzerland, Paris, China, London. His confusion metastasized into fear. He mumbled the word "gypsy" over and over.

His nightmare worsened. He heard the voices of both Martha and Mary—his wife, and the woman he was having an affair with.

When he opened his eyes, the nightmare came to life.

"Well, this is awkward."

"Another drunken accident, Ernest?" Martha snapped in disgust.

"Ah, my favorite fan..."

"You will never change."

"Always so supportive, Martha. Sorry to have disappointed you by surviving. You've lost the opportunity to play the grieving widow. Think of the stories you could have written."

"You disgust me, Ernest Hemmingway." She turned to Mary. "Good luck with him, honey. He's all yours."

As Martha stormed out of the room, Mary fluffed Hemingway's pillow and tucked in his covers.

"What happened to the old woman?" he asked her.

"What old woman, Papa?"

CHAPTER 28

NIGHT BEFORE BATTLE

1944

An artificial dawn erupted at precisely 0545. Naval guns boomed in unison as if announcing the end of the world. And for many it was just that, as the salvos rained death and destruction upon the German positions on the beaches of Normandy.

Hemingway thought he had seen all that war had to show him, but he had never witnessed a naval bombardment. The rounds lit the sky in reverse, from the ocean not the stars. Thousands of white-hot muzzle flashes popped like the bulbs of paparazzi. Each baritone rumble from the big sixteen-inch guns announced that an eighteen-hundred-pound high explosive shell was on its way. Blinding lights pierced the pre-dawn darkness, and debilitating noises concussed the fleeing night. All of it wrapped man, machine, and the dawning day in confusion. Thousands of guns letting loose hell, the thunderous salvos giving way to rolling thunder as the gunners lost cadence. Constant lightning crashed on the beach, penetrating the building cloud of smoke and dust. Ships soon became obscured in a cordite fog, pulsating as shells continued to be hurled toward Omaha Beach.

On board the *USS Dorothea Dix*, AP-67, Hemingway watched the shells impact the defenses through giant naval binoculars. For a moment they looked almost like the fireflies gathered in the tall grass around Walloon Lake—a memory from his youth. It was strange how perception could be so disassociated from reality.

He shifted his attention to the infantrymen flooding over the sides of the ship. They clung to cargo nets like insects, descending to the LVCP landing craft below. Timing their leaps to the twenty-foot swells, they filled the small, pitching Higgins boats. The men already onboard encouraged the ones who came after, pulled in those who mistimed their jumps, and got out of the way of the ones who crashed onto the flat bottoms. Each man was laden with heavy combat gear, and to go overboard meant certain death by drowning.

When full, the LCVP landing craft and its thirty-six soldiers would move away and allow an empty one to come alongside and repeat the process. The full LVCPs were already circling, forming a swarm.

Soon the LVCPs moved toward the beach. Their flat bottoms caused them to pitch and yaw. Nervous stomachs surrendered their breakfasts, and the stench of vomit mixed with the toxic diesel fumes of the Gray Marine 6-71 engine. The relentless thunder of guns pounded the men's senses.

Forty minutes after it started, the bombardment ceased. God's sun broke in the heavens above the man-made dawn of hell. Currents tore at the formation of LCVPs, and the line broke. Bedlam followed as some landing craft reached the beach early while others ran aground on sandbars a hundred yards out.

Front ramps dropped, and entire boatloads of men were vaporized in a pink mist generated by thousands of machine gun rounds, without having taken even a single step from the landing craft. Others ran off into deep water and were dragged to the sandy bottom by their gear and drowned. Still others struggled ashore, where they hid behind the steel landing obstacles. Wave after wave of troops hit Omaha Beach, where thousands would soon lie dead or wounded.

It was after the fifth wave that Hemingway and the other correspondents closed on the beach themselves. He tried to hold his binoculars to his eyes, but as the LCVP bounced from swell to swell, they banged against his bandaged wound. Cursing, he focused them on the lines of dead lying on the sands.

Heavy bullets slammed into the front ramp, and shells burst on the ocean around them, showering him and the others in salt water. The coxswain spun the wheel violently and turned the Higgins boat around.

"Where the hell are you going, Petty Officer?" Hemingway raged in disbelief.

"Back to the fleet, sir."

"But the war is that way!" Hemingway shouted furiously, pointing at the beach.

"Those are my orders if we came under fire. And in case you haven't noticed, we *have* come under fire. All due respect, sir."

Hemingway threw the binoculars onto the deck in frustration. He turned to watch the receding beach and saw a LCVP disappear under a direct hit.

All those men gone in the blink of an eye, he thought. *Nothing left, nothing to send home. It's as if they never existed.* He felt the shame of fleeing to relative safety. *I should be on that beach. I should be fighting for France.*

CHAPTER 29

THE CAPITAL OF THE WORLD

1944

Paratroopers rained from the sky inland on D-Day, then consolidated, holding large areas as the landing troops pushed toward them. Reeling on multiple fronts, the German command fought with what they could, while Hitler waited for Patton and his fictitious army at Calais. The emperor had clothes—it was a brain he lacked.

By July, Hemingway had joined up with Colonel Charles "Buck" Lanham's Twenty-Second Infantry Regiment, attached to the Second Armor Division. With the airborne units leading the way, Second Armor secured the Cotentin Peninsula that held the landing beaches. Once the Allied Forces had established a secure beachhead, supply piers were built in the bays, and both supplies and reinforcements with heavy vehicles and tanks flooded into France.

By August, the Twenty-Second had attached to the Fourth Infantry Division in its drive toward Paris. They bivouacked in Rambouillet to rest for the final push. Hemingway was sitting in the command tent with Colonel Lanham when a small, scruffy, very nervous Frenchman entered, escorted by a captain from the Free French Second Armored Division.

"Colonel, this is Corporal René LaFleur of the Resistance," said the captain. "He can detail positions of the German defenses."

"Corporal?" Lanham replied. "Where is your captain? Your sergeant?"

The captain translated the question, and was about to translate the response when Hemingway beat him to it.

"Dead."

Charts were spread out, and LaFleur detailed positions and weaknesses. After his briefing, he walked out, and Hemingway followed.

"Monsieur LaFleur," he said. He spoke to the man in his native tongue. "Do you need help in your unit? I am experienced in leading men in battle."

"*Oui*, Monsieur Hemingway. Your reputation precedes you."

"Might we fight our way into Paris discreetly?"

LaFleur smiled, showing tobacco-stained teeth. "To be first to liberate Paris?"

Hemingway returned the smile. "Why not, René? Why not?"

Machine gun fire raked their position, Hemingway and LaFleur sought refuge behind a fallen tree. Rounds impacted, kicking up chunks of rotted wood and moss.

"Shall we rush the machine gun nest?" LaFleur asked.

"No, it will just get good men killed. Take two men as far east as you can, then move forward. I will do the same to the west. Once we are past the machine gun position, we will curl back and come up from behind them."

Each group low-crawled to the flanks of the nest. They took advantage of the forest, using the foliage as cover. And when they were behind the Germans, they simply walked up to their rear and shot them in their backs.

Hemingway stood in the open, his Thompson submachine gun still smoking. His men cheered him. Paris was being abandoned by the Germans, and these poor fools left to slow the advance were dying quickly.

*   *   *

In Clamart, they commandeered three trucks and sped toward Issy-les-Moulineaux. There Hemingway found a motorcycle and sidecar, as well as a stash of champagne. As he loaded the champagne into the sidecar, a local told him that the Spanish had liberated Paris the night before.

"The Spanish?" said a dumbfounded Hemingway.

"*Oui*, Monsieur. The colonne Dronne, Ninth Armored Company. They are veterans of the Spanish Civil War."

Hemingway let out a howl of laughter. "So we finally win against the fascists!"

*   *   *

Undeterred, the determined ragtag warriors set their sights on liberating a new target: the Ritz. LaFleur drove the motorcycle with Hemingway in the sidecar. As they sped toward the Seine with abandon, they rounded a corner and found themselves facing a charging Panzer tank. While its gun boomed, Hemingway stood in the sidecar and blasted away with his Thompson. Heavy machine gun rounds impacted all around him. Death was certain.

Suddenly the tank veered to its right flank to engage a regular army unit. A pair of bazookas swooshed, and the Panzer died like a gassed bug.

LaFleur revved the engine and swerved around the tank. The Seine was in sight! At full speed they turned onto the quai de Grenelle. As they passed the Eiffel Tower, Hemingway popped open a bottle of champagne, drank from it, and handed it to LaFleur.

They crossed the Seine, weaved through traffic, and dodged past the rejoicing crowds on the rue Royale. An occasional rifle fired in the distance as they made a hard right turn on rue Saint Honoré, then a left on Place Vendôme. They screeched to a stop in front of the Hotel Ritz.

Hemingway stepped from the sidecar like a conquering emperor, the butt of his Thompson perched on his right hip, a bottle of champagne in his left hand. He strutted toward the stone edifice with his men close behind, all of them armed to the teeth. Hand grenades dangled from web gear, ammunition belts hung around their necks, and pistols, rifles, and machine guns were slung over shoulders. Their appearance contrasted sharply with the elegance of the Ritz.

* * *

It was summer in Paris, and Hemingway was in full bloom. He sat with his French irregulars, the former resistance, in one of the Ritz's glass rooms. Arched iron beams held panes of glass over the stone pavement on the side of the hotel. Two identical structures were separated by an open-air veranda. The irregulars sipped wine and snacked on cheese and bread.

Colonel Buck Lanham jumped from a jeep and stormed onto the portico, waving a letter. When he reached Hemingway's table, he slammed it onto the white tablecloth.

"Damn it, Papa, I told you to stay out of the field!"

"What is this, Buck?"

"Some pipsqueak asshole reporter filed charges against you."

"For what?"

Lanham waved his hand around to include all the irregulars in his scope. "Violating the Geneva Convention by leading troops in combat as a correspondent."

Hemingway laughed heartily in response. He took a pull off his whiskey and replied, "Millions dead, and some weasel wants me charged?"

"This is serious, Papa."

"What is? My observation of this fine group of Frenchmen, offering occasional advice from my years of experience as a war correspondent?"

"He has pictures of you with the weapons." Buck pointed to the Thompson leaning against Hemingway's wrought-iron chair.

LaFleur spoke quickly, boldly. "That is merely a gift. A… how do you say in English?"

"A souvenir," said Hemingway.

"Yes. A souvenir."

Lanham frowned. "You will swear to that, in a sworn statement?"

"Of course," said LaFleur. "All of us will."

LaFleur spoke to the men in rapid fire, then wrote out a statement on the back of the same letter that charged Hemingway. Each man signed the statement, and LaFleur handed it to Colonel Lanham.

He looked it over. "Well, this is good enough for me—not sure of the chain of command though. Patton is still mad as hell you beat him to Paris." He folded the paper and shoved it in a pocket. "But no more observing!"

"Papa!" called a voice.

Hemingway looked up to see Pablo Picasso running across the sidewalk. "Pablo!"

The men embraced, shouting over each other.

Lanham threw up his hands and left.

CHAPTER 30

A MOVABLE FEAST

1944

Colonel Johan Schrict had enthusiastically executed the orders for the Final Solution. He personally saw to it that thousands of Jews and undesirables were rounded up and sent to the death camps. SS storm troopers had worked at a frenetic pace as the Americans closed on Paris.

But once the rail cars were assigned to relieving France of the spoils of war, it was time to move on. Paintings, sculpture, art of all kinds was being looted. Killing innocent people just had to take a back seat.

Besides, he had no interest in standing his ground in the defense of Paris. Moving quickly to the rear was certainly a sounder policy.

As his staff car proceeded north to Germany, he watched reinforcements pass without much thought. After all, he was an administrator, not a warrior. Himmler himself had summoned him to Wewelsburg Castle, SS headquarters.

He glanced at the skull ring of the SS—he had been given it after a Teutonic ceremony at Wewelsburg—and rubbed it absently with a thumb. He was a true believer in the cult of death.

Rotating his wrist to reveal the fine Swiss watch he had picked out of the confiscation inventory, he noted it was past 1500. He uncorked a bottle of Krug champagne, 1928, his favorite, and poured it into a tall flute—one chosen so he could drink on the ride even while being jostled in his staff car. But there was no need; the open-air Mercedes-Benz W31-type G4 was a shining example of German engineering, so smooth he didn't spill a drop.

A second glass sat in the basket; he tossed it dismissively from the car. It had been for his French girl, who had disappeared the day before. No matter. As an SS colonel he'd have his pick of German girls.

Reclining, he basked in the beautiful August day while sipping the sparkling champagne. Thoughts of his chance meeting with the Führer all those years ago ran through his mind. From mopping up puke in a beer hall, to enjoying fine wine and cheese on his way to meet one of the most powerful men in the world.

Reaching across the seat, Schrict patted the alligator suitcase. Like his jackboots, it shone brightly in the sun. He was a prideful man, and it showed.

Perhaps Herr Himmler will like my stories, he mused.

CHAPTER 31

DEATH IN THE AFTERNOON

1944

When the war started, he had been one of the most feared and hated men in Siberia: Stalin's number one henchman. Colonel Petrovski was indifferent to death—Russian or German, it didn't matter to him.

He was now assigned to rid Germany of the Nazis. And in his normal zeal, he had decided *all* Germans were Nazis. It was an excuse for excess—rape, pillage, and plunder—but not what motivated him. His motivation was the deed in and of itself. Only those who were weak of will needed an excuse.

His command sergeant approached. A slack-jawed moron with an IQ barely above imbecile. He was, however, quite useful. Like Petrovski, he didn't flinch at the infliction of cruelty.

LELAND C. SHANLE JR.

"Comrade Colonel, Major Stanislaw requests you come."

Petrovski rose from his makeshift table and followed Sergeant Putin through the rubble of Berlin to the front line. Dust and the acrid smell of war hung in the air.

They came upon Stanislaw, who was crouching over the nearly headless body of an SS colonel. The dead man lay on top of an alligator suitcase, embracing it awkwardly, his dead hand still clinging to the handle.

"Booby trapped?" Petrovski asked.

Stanislaw shook his head. "We just cleared it."

Petrovski peeled the lifeless fingers off the handle and jerked the bag from underneath the corpse. The dead colonel's face flopped against the concrete as it rolled off the suitcase.

Petrovski handed the case to Putin. "Take it to my tent. We shall see exactly what was so important to this Nazi."

*   *   *

The wind whipped, and Petrovski threw another scrap of wood in the barrel that warmed the small tent. He waved at the smoke and turned up the oil lamp just slightly, not wanting to attract the attention of a sniper.

As he opened the suitcase, a cold breeze snapped the tent's flap, startling him. But he quickly returned his attention to the contents.

He shuffled through the manuscripts aimlessly—until he spotted the name *Hemingway*. He had read Hemingway back in the twenties, before the author—along with all other American authors—was blacklisted. What were Hemingway's manuscripts doing here in Berlin?

As he continued to rifle through the contents, he found other manuscripts, newer ones, penned in German. He knew enough

German to recognize that they were copies of the Hemingway manuscripts. But why? And why had the SS colonel guarded these old manuscripts with his life?

"Sergeant!"

"Yes, Comrade Colonel?"

"Tell Major Stanislaw I want a file on the SS colonel by morning."

"Yes, Comrade."

Petrovski sensed that Putin used the word "comrade" as a slight. But Petrovski was a political officer, and held his tongue.

He received the dossier on the SS colonel at first light. But dossier was far too strong a word—they knew very little about the man, other than that he had been assigned to Paris.

So Petrovski went to what was left of the Berlin Library, intending to find what he could about Hemingway. The place was a shambles. The roof was open to the morning sun, and books were strewn across the floor. An old woman was collecting some of the books in a small wooden wheelbarrow—no doubt planning to burn them for warmth. A babushka—more of a rag, like the clothes that hung from her—almost hid her white braid. Curiously, she reminded Petrovski of his own mother.

He stepped over books and broken shelves until he got to the proper aisle. Strangely, the shelf containing Hemingway's books was upright, making it easy for him to collect them all and shove them in his rucksack.

He went back the way he had come. As he approached the old woman, he slipped his TT-33 pistol out of its holster, pressed it to her head, and pulled the trigger. He didn't even wait to see the withered body fall.

* * *

Three days later, after reading all of Hemingway's published work—and considering the German translations and carbon copies— he concluded that the manuscripts in the suitcase were unpublished. And when he came across an article about the lost suitcase, he had no doubt. A rare smile crossed his face.

It seems I will be a great author after all.

CHAPTER 32

RENATA

Hemingway and Mary married and returned to Cuba. In January he began a new novel, *The Garden of Eden*. By June he had written eight hundred pages, but his progress stalled after the death of Gertrude Stein in July.

He was beginning to feel old. Many of his writer friends were gone: Yeats, Ford, Fitzgerald, Anderson, Joyce, and now Stein. Her passing rattled his feeling of immortality. But it was the headaches that drove him from the pen—and they only worsened after another car wreck, another concussion.

They traveled to Europe in 1948. The farther he moved from war, the older he felt. Like the ruined cities on the Continent, he struggled to rebuild. To return to his former glory. Dark thoughts crept into his consciousness.

A pilgrimage to Fossalta, Italy, where he was wounded in 1918, felt more like a funeral procession. He felt that his life, instead of ending in a blaze of glory, was instead diminishing to insignificance. *I must get my essence back*, he thought. Esto vir. *Be a man.*

Dawn broke over the Trieste province, relieving the chill that filled the duck blind. Jagged hills ran all the way to the Adriatic's edge. Shots rang out from the small group of hunters, a duck fluttered and fell, and a retriever leapt on command.

Hemingway's head pounded. He was suffering from a hangover.

He turned to see the breaking sun bathe a goddess in its golden light. Captivated, infatuated, he could not stop staring at her. He was lovestruck by her beauty and grace. And when Adriana Ivancich turned and gave him a Mona Lisa smile, his surrender was complete.

Later, at the Piazza Unita d'Italia and its fountains, punctuated by the noon sun's illumination, she sat before him, the beauty and grace of God. Just a few miles away was the darkness of man, the Iron Curtain. Hemingway considered the juxtaposition, the peril of Trieste, of this relationship.

An old woman leaned on a cane nearby, her hair braided tightly. Hemingway didn't notice. His attention, his concentration, was singular. Adriana was perfect, as if pulled from the ceiling of the Sistine Chapel. His obsession with her was dangerous, titillating, forbidden. She was nineteen, younger than his own children.

Thus he fled to Cortina with Mary. She sensed there was a reason, but she said nothing. In Cortina she broke her ankle skiing. Without distraction, his fixation returned. Hemingway's love affair with Adriana caused friction with Mary, but it was a platonic relationship only. He wanted it that way; it gave the relationship dignity.

Unable to exorcise his passions, he wrote with a fury. *Across the River and Into the Trees* was penned, with Colonel Buck Lanham as its main character, and Adriana as the forbidden teenage love. Hemingway named her character *Renata*, which meant reborn. Unrequited love was its theme, wrapped by the duality of death. The existential truth, that life is more amplified by its proximity to death, was its message. Adriana herself designed the book's cover.

To celebrate the publication, Hemingway invited her and her mother to Cuba. But caustic reviews preceded her arrival, and he was furious. To make matters worse, by the time she got there, their relationship had become public. Renata was revealed.

Adriana found him on the veranda, looking down on the lights of Havana. Mary had already told her of the reviews and his mood.

She quietly walked up behind where he sat. "*Ego te provoco.*"

He took a drink from the tumbler he held. "You challenge me?"

"*Esto quod es.*"

"I am, if nothing else, true to myself, Adriana."

"*Litter ex animo.*"

He contemplated her words. *Write from the soul.* Had he not done precisely that all these years? Had he become shallow? Too transparent? That critics could see through his work so easily…

The writing, he knew, was exceptional, but was it from his soul? Had his soul been chipped away over the years, diminished? Hollywood had pumped out six more films based on his past work since the war started, but *Across the River* was the only literary work he'd done.

He stood, his eyes still on Havana. "*Resurgam, litter scripta manet.*"

CHAPTER 33

THE SEA CHANGE

1951

Finca Vigia awoke to a flurry of activity. Hemingway had servants loading luggage and had sent his first mate to the Pilar to ready it for an extended journey.

Mary stepped out of their room, pulling a robe tight. "Papa, what's going on?"

"We're going to where the devil got my fish."

"What?"

Adriana and her mother came out of their rooms with sleepy looks of confusion. But Hemingway was energized; he felt ten years younger. He felt vigor, hope, his head clear of pain.

"I must write real, from the soul," he explained. "So we are going to where the devil and I fought. Bimini."

* * *

Hemingway wrote with a fury he hadn't felt since the early days of Paris, and with a discipline he hadn't had since Key West. Eight weeks later he walked onto the veranda overlooking the ocean with two copies of his manuscript. He handed one to Mary and the other to Adriana.

In the light of the setting sun, they read the title: *The Old Man and the Sea.*

"It's the best I can write, ever, for all my life."

Both women gazed into his intense eyes as he looked from one to the other. They then began to read. Hemingway mixed a drink and then leaned on the rail to watch the setting sun.

"Did you see it?" he asked them excitedly.

"See what, Papa?"

"The green flash! I always thought it was an old sailors' tale. All these years on the sea, I've never seen it."

"Really? Are you teasing us?" Adriana said.

"It was an intense flash of green, for just a microsecond. If I had blinked, I would have missed it. It was amazing. Beautiful."

* * *

He awoke feeling weakened. He remembered this feeling. Italy, in the hospital, 1918, after he had lost so much blood.

Kicking his feet over the side of the bed, he poured himself a cool glass of water from the bedside pitcher. With a shaking hand he drank it all down and sat quietly listening to the surf.

He heard a sniffle, and turned to see Mary weeping in a soft leather chair. The lamp was on, even though the mid-morning sun was streaming into the room through big open windows.

"Have you been up all night, Mary?"

She wiped a tear from her eye with a silk handkerchief. "It is your best."

"The manuscript?"

"Yes. It is poetry in prose. I… I couldn't stop until it was done."

He picked her up from the chair in a soft swooping motion and carried her, like a groom would carry his bride, to bed. They made love in the sunlight, and then she fell asleep.

Hemingway found Adriana and her mother in the open-air living room seated on rattan furniture. He poured a coffee from the silver service and sat with them.

"What did you think?" he asked.

"I fell asleep after a few chapters," said Adriana, "but what I read was quite nice."

He nodded, pushed away the cup and saucer, and went to the bar to mix a Bloody Mary.

The Old Man and the Sea was published in September of 1952. It was his biggest success. Five million copies were printed, and they sold out in two days. It was featured in *Life* magazine and was made into a Book of the Month Club selection in May of 1953. And most importantly, it won the Pulitzer Prize for Literature. With this novel, Ernest Hemingway had achieved international celebrity status. In a few short months his critics went from announcing his career over to proclaiming his genius.

CHAPTER 34

WINNER TAKE NOTHING

1953

Colonel Petrovski stood with pride as Comrade Turchin, a KGB general, absently paged through his manuscript.

The windows rattled from a Siberian-born gust, and the general looked up. He watched the late March snow blow sideways past the window. A problem lay on the concealed second desktop, and it had just solved itself.

In the Soviet Union, every desk had two tops. One top was four inches below the actual desktop, and was used to quickly hide documents if someone entered your office unexpectedly. There were many secrets in the Soviet world. Paranoia was a national trait, a way of life, not a psychological condition.

The problem was this. Stalin was dead, and his henchmen, the Purgers, had become an embarrassment to the new, "enlightened" leadership. Thus it was that the letter on the second desktop demanded that Turchin rid the Soviet Union of Petrovski.

He snapped closed the means to do it, pressed a red button on the underside of his desk, and stood with feigned rage and indignation. As armed guards rushed in, he threw the manuscript at Petrovski.

"This is subversive! Arrest the traitor!"

Petrovski would have rotted in Lubyanka Prison, but the temperature prevented it. Like old vegetables, he lay in cold storage. Former comrades abandoned him in the blink of an eye. No one came to his defense. His visitor log was blank. Even his wife and children stood aside without a word of defense or support.

The German translations did not help his case—not that anything could have. They made for great theater at Petrovski's show trial. He was denounced as an enemy of the Soviet Union.

A conviction, while never in doubt in a Soviet political trial, was handed down with demonstrative flair. Evidence was recorded, collated, and packed away for storage in the basement at KGB Headquarters. There it would sit, ready for an appeal that everyone knew would never come.

Petrovski was sentenced to a Siberian gulag for re-education—and to rededicate himself to the Soviet cause. He was packed into an unheated box car with other dissidents. His long train of misery pulled out of the prisoners' station, bound for the frozen wasteland. They were packed in so tightly no one could sit. There were no facilities, and even in the frigid conditions the stench was unbearable.

General Turchin had wanted a death sentence. In Soviet Russia, it was never wise to leave an enemy alive. This often meant children, too. But the enlightened leadership of the new Kremlin would not allow it. Turchin addressed the potential problem by stripping Petrovski's uniform of all rank and insignia, but ordering that he was to remain in it. Even stripped, it was unmistakably the uniform of a KGB officer. And then he signed orders sending Petrovski to an area of Siberia that Petrovski had personally purged.

Turchin had no doubt the Petrovski problem would be solved soon.

Heated only by the bodies of its inhabitants, the train plowed east. It stopped only for coal, once a day. Water for its steam engine was provided by the prisoners shoveling snow into the tank, where it was melted. If prisoners lingered too long near the heat of the engine, they were motivated by the butt of a rifle.

It grew colder the further east they traveled. Stale, moldy bread and handfuls of snow sustained them as days turned to weeks. Dirty gray sunlight seeping through cracks marked the days, absolute darkness the nights.

A shrill whistle ended the monotony. The train of sadness and desperation ended its journey. Petrovski contemplated the reversal of his life. A dissident? He had spent his life crushing dissent, exterminating even the slightest sign of free thought.

And not just free thought—*all* thought. By showing the manuscript, though, he had condemned himself. The irony of it was not lost on him.

Sliding down from the train car into the bleak camp was soul-crushing. Even for a pitiless man who had never before demonstrated that he possessed one.

Low clouds hung over dirty snow, and a frigid breeze swirled ice crystals around him. His nose hair froze and his eyes watered. He surveyed his surroundings. *This is the Soviet: no art, no literature, no love or beauty, no hope. This is what I served. Perhaps I can endear myself to the Zampolite by becoming an informant.*

His thoughts were interrupted by the gulag prisoners, who had formed a ring around him. There was recognition in their hate-filled eyes. Sensing danger, he looked past them for the guards. Their backs were turned. They were walking away.

Inching forward, the doomed moved as one. Closing the ring, pressing toward him. Hands ripped at his clothes. Fingernails tore at exposed flesh. A low murmur, like a Gregorian chant, then an old woman's shriek, a frenzied call for blood. Hands opened and closed.

Little hand, the little hand.

It wasn't dirt that fell from the grasping hands; it was hair, skin, and muscle. Blood sanctified the primordial rite and turned the snow red. Boiling like a cauldron, the mob surged and ebbed, each member wanting its own piece.

Excruciating pain was Petrovski's only cogent thought. In all his life's work, he was sure he had never been able to inflict such a crescendo of agony.

A small, wrinkled hand, with long jagged fingernails, dug into his carotid artery and tore it open. When it sprayed the mob, they were at last sated. They moved back, allowing his devoured corpse to collapse into the snow and mud.

The owner of the jagged fingernails pulled the babushka from her head. A white braid fell free as she wiped the blood from her face.

From a guard tower, the camp commandant watched the steaming blood mix with the muddy snow, snuffing as it froze. He shrugged. Just another day in the workers' paradise.

CHAPTER 35

AN AFRICAN STORY

1953

Hemingway chased his youth to Africa. He ran from weakness, age, the inevitable. His mind had given him one last glory, but his body was betraying him. Failing him. He was not content to be condemned as a voyeur in the struggle of life and death. And he knew only one way to get back into the fight: Africa.

Mary stirred in the tent. Hemingway checked the pot of coffee he had on the fire. It began to percolate, throbbing to life like the African plain.

Life and death surrounded him. There were endless ways to die here. An elephant, a hippopotamus, a lion, or something as small as a snake or insect. All could end his life in an instant. He loved Africa for this, its primordial struggle.

He reached across the fire and picked up his rifle. Sliding back the bolt, he inspected the cartridge and re-chambered it. He clicked on the safety and set it next to his chair. He did the same inspection of his holstered .44 revolver.

A morning chill hung in the air. He pulled up the collar on his khaki hunting jacket, then bent to re-tie his knee-high brown leather boots—protection against venomous fangs.

Mary emerged from the tent, and he poured her a cup from the pot. She accepted the steaming liquid with a smile.

He sat back down in the camp chair and set his own cup down on a folding table. He doused the gas lantern that hissed at the coming morning, then closed the notebook he had been writing in.

"Do you ever wonder where that suitcase went?" Mary asked.

"Good God, woman, what made you think of that?"

"I dreamt of it last night. A strange, troubling dream…"

A twig cracked, and Hemingway grabbed his pistol as he spun to face the dark bush. Kilimanjaro flashed red where the sun broke the horizon and lit its snow-capped peak.

A familiar voice from the bush: "It's me, Papa."

"Ah, Philip. Come, join us."

Hemingway handed Philip Percival a hot cup of coffee.

"Thank you, Papa. We need to move quickly. A herd of antelope will cross the Orangi River before noon. We must position ourselves before then."

Percival had brought them to the chokepoint of a narrow valley. It funneled down to the river. A perfect spot to bag a trophy.

* * *

Moving as one, the herd stampeded into the Orangi's valley. They moved like a fast-moving mudflow, a single entity broken only by straight, spiraled antlers that pointed toward the late morning sky. As they crashed into the water, it frothed like a shaken beer. Crocodiles slid from their mud perches to join them.

Percival spoke. "They will cross very quickly. Mary, aim for one on the edge so it won't be trampled after you drop it. Papa, we will wait for the vanguard."

"The vanguard?"

"Yes, the young bucks who guard the rear of the herd. Their racks will not be broken yet from challenging to lead, and their meat will be tender."

"Sounds like a plan."

"Our shot will come and go fast as the dust clears. They will storm past us quickly."

Crocodiles surfaced, waiting for a mistake. And they got one. A calf stumbled and rolled down the slope and into the water, outside the protective perimeter of the herd. With amazing power, a twelve-foot croc pulsed its tail and struck in an instant. A vise of teeth clamped on the flailing calf and dragged it under.

"One more thing," Percival shouted over the approaching thunder, "we are not hunting alone." He nodded toward a pride of lions lurking in the scrub. "If the lions spook them this way, everyone stand up and fire your rifles in the air, so we won't be trampled."

Mary glanced nervously at Hemingway, and he returned her glance with a smile and a wink, extracting a smile from her in return.

Mary took a bead on a male; she dropped her trophy with a single shot. Hemingway was wide-eyed with excitement as the herd rushed by just below their perch. It reminded him of the running of the bulls in Pamplona.

Dust rose thick, obscuring the herd. Pounding hooves generated an intense noise that built to a cacophony before tapering. There, in the diminishing tendrils of dust, Hemingway saw his target. Jumping to his feet for a clear shot, he pulled the trigger.

The butt of the rifle stabbed his shoulder, the explosion rang in his ears, and cordite stung his nose. He stood as the cloud dissipated, revealing four antelopes dead on the Serengeti.

Their competition, the pride, had claimed two of them. Perhaps they were old or weak, but without the vanguard they had been easy prey. Wary of the human presence, the lions dragged their meal into the brush. A hyena poked its scraggly head around a bush, but Percival shot close enough to scare it off.

"Nice shot, both of you," he said. "Let's go see what we have."

The antelope's eyes stared up at Hemingway with neither accusation or defeat. The beast had struggled, fought, and lost. No more, no less.

Percival pivoted its head, holding each horn. "It's a fantastic animal, Papa."

"Truly magnificent," Hemingway whispered. "It will go home with us."

*   *   *

Stars flickered as they had for millions of years over a Serengeti Plain that had changed little in that time. It was the mystery of Africa, why it was stuck in time. Its beauty and danger were unsurpassed anywhere in the world. Europe, the Orient, even the young Americas had been tamed, but not Mother Africa. She alone stood defiantly. Man had started here, and even with all those millennia behind him, he could not rob her of her dignity.

Wondrous smells wafted from the fire, where back strap and other prime cuts roasted over the acacia coals. Lean meat gave up just enough fat to feed the fire, making it sizzle and crack.

Hemingway stood gazing at the heavens, and Percival came to join him.

"Better stay closer to the fire, Papa. We don't want to invite problems the night before we leave."

"Look at the stars, Philip. They are different here."

"Yes, they are. They have held me all these years. Look at Kilimanjaro."

Hemingway looked across the low fire licking at the darkness. A full moon bathed Kilimanjaro's crown an ivory white.

"I will write of this," he said, "and they will think it fiction."

"Better that they do, Papa, otherwise they'd come. That would ruin it."

"Yes. It is best left to men like us."

CHAPTER 36

ACROSS THE RIVER AND INTO THE TREES

1954

Hemingway sat in the co-pilot seat of the Cessna 170 as they circled Murchison Falls. Uganda's breathtaking lakes and waterfalls were best seen from the air. Mary's camera chattered from the back.

"Take her down, Roy, let's get a good look," Hemingway shouted over the Continental C145-2 engine.

At Murchison Falls, the half-mile-wide Victoria Nile was compressed into a thirty-foot-wide gorge, and then it dropped fifty feet. The energy release was incredible; even from here, Hemingway could hear the roar.

A flock of birds materialized in their face. The pilot, Roy, knew the 170 would not fly, even at full power, if they lost the windscreen. Simple aerodynamics wouldn't allow it. He dove the aircraft over the falls to get under the flock.

But he hadn't seen the telegraph wire stretched across the gorge. It grabbed the engine cowl, and the left wing. Pulled to its tinsel strength, the wire snapped with a crack like the report of a shotgun. Now twisted, the wing fought to throw them from the air instead of lifting them gently into it. Oil from the compromised engine splattered the windscreen.

Succumbing to the forces of physics, the Cessna slammed into the trees along the shoreline of the Victoria Nile below the falls. The howl of the engine was replaced by the sound of snapping trees and twisting metal.

* * *

Hemingway blinked himself to consciousness.

It took him a moment to realize he was looking at the smashed fuselage of the Cessna. He rolled over and flinched when he brushed his forehead. Memory of the crash flooded back with the spike of pain—but he recalled nothing after impact. It was like coming off a major bender; he remembered only bits and pieces, and struggled to put it all back together.

"You had to ride in the front," Mary said. She had knelt down beside him.

"Hello, Mary. And how are you?"

She clutched her ribs and smiled through a grimace. "You hit your head on the dashboard."

"I believe they call it a glare shield, my dear."

160

Mary couldn't help but laugh, even though it caused stabs of pain. She helped him up gingerly, and they walked together to the water's edge, where Roy sat.

The pilot held out a bottle of whiskey. "Thank God it survived! How's the head, Papa?"

"Just peachy. And you?"

"Banged up a bit, but none the worse for wear, considering."

"So what's our plan? The radio?"

"Smashed, I'm afraid. It wouldn't do us much good this low anyway. But we should be fine. Eventually a tour boat will be along to see the falls from below. Until then, we fish, boil some water to drink..."

"And when darkness comes?"

"Well, that could be an issue. Big animals will come to this pool to drink. I think we need to get up on one of the ledges overlooking the falls."

Roy had a survival kit: hatchet, fishing gear, tarp, and a 1911 .45-caliber pistol. After stacking a supply of firewood and erecting a lean-to, the three survivors settled down to roast fish on a stick over the fire.

Darkness brought the sounds of Africa close, but fortunately most were muffled by the sound of the falls. Only those creatures curious enough to investigate the fire could be heard. Smelling the humans, they kept a safe distance.

At sunrise, they watched the hippos and elephants bathe in the pool below. It was a wondrous sight, and Mary captured them through her camera's lens. The animals returned again at sunset. But as the sun disappeared again, Hemingway began to worry.

After another cold breakfast of fish, they decided to break camp and wait by the wreckage. Roy assured them today they would be rescued. Sure enough, at midday a tour boat came around a bend. Roy shot a flare, and their ordeal ended.

By late afternoon they were in a twin engine de Havilland Dragon Rapide, bound for Entebbe and medical attention. It had a big cabin that sat eight passengers. The flight would be full.

"You sit in the back this time, Papa."

He laughed. "Okay, Mary. Okay."

Coughing to life, the de Havilland Gypsy Six inline engine whipped at the red dirt and swirled it behind the bi-winged bush plane. A second engine came to life and did the same.

Reginald Cartwright, the pilot, revved the engines, moving his heavily loaded craft out of the red dust cloud. He pivoted around the left main tire at the end of the dirt runway, ran both Gypsies to takeoff power, and released the brakes.

Hemingway sensed the acceleration was too slow.

Fat tires seemed to dig into the loose earth. Reginald pushed the power up to full. The Gypsies wailed. Finally, the tail came up, but the brush at the airstrip's end seemed close—very close. The Rapide began to skip on and off the runway. It rotated into the air just as the left Gypsy engine came apart.

A connecting rod broke and pierced the engine block. Hot oil filled the nacelle housing the engine. Even from his seat, Hemingway could see the flames clawing their way out of the nacelle.

Reginald fought for control. The right Gypsy screeched at emergency power. But weight, heat, and the inadequate speed conspired against them. Airflow separated from the left wing, and it stopped producing lift. It stalled, causing the aircraft to roll into the bad engine.

Screaming, tearing, crunching accompanied the aircraft's violent return to earth. The left wing struck the ground first. It tore open, spilling fuel, which ignited. And then all noise ceased but for the whimpering, the sobbing, and the crackling of the fire.

Hemingway saw Reginald pulling Mary out the cockpit door. But the cabin door was stuck. He threw his shoulder into it. Pain struck like 220 volts of electricity. He was trapped, the fire expanding.

He heard shrieking—and then a low cackle. Through the flames he saw an old woman, flickering in and out of view.

He hammered at the door, with first his fist and then his skull. Finally it gave. He rolled out, followed by two more passengers.

Reginald grabbed his safari jacket by the collar and pulled him clear.

"The damn Gypsy didn't get me!" Hemingway shouted. "That bitch didn't get me!"

They fell to the ground as the Rapide was completely consumed by the pyre.

Reginald faced Hemingway and shouted above the din. "How did you know this aircraft had Gypsy engines?"

Hemingway fell unconscious.

CHAPTER 37

UNDER KILIMANJARO

1954

A fractured skull leaked fluid, a dislocated shoulder was reset, a broken back put in traction. Internal injuries complicated the treatment. Hemingway awoke temporarily blind, momentarily terrified.

"You *had* to ride in the back, didn't you, Papa?"

He recognized Mary's voice but could only manage to crack a slight smile.

He healed—slowly—but he would never be pain-free again. His only amusement during this time was reading his own obituaries.

After his release from the Nairobi hospital, they recuperated in the Stanley Hotel. But fame from his Pulitzer and surviving not one, but two aircraft crashes, hounded him. Surly and in pain, he sought refuge at Percival's lodge on the Tsavo Plain.

* * *

After weeks of lying about, Hemingway had convinced Percival he could return to the bush. He felt it would rejuvenate him.

And so it was that Percival tore open the tent flap.

"Papa, Mary, get up quickly!" There was alarm in his voice.

"What is it?"

"Wildfire!"

They dressed quickly and emerged from the tent to see the porters and Percival looking south. A deep orange line stood on the horizon, worthy of any coming sunrise. But it was to the south, and at midnight.

Hemingway studied it through binoculars. It pulsed red, with large orange plums leaping into the dark skies. It reminded him of looking at the sun through a filtered telescope. Fueled by dry brush and fanned by a strong southerly wind, it was moving dangerously fast.

"Do we outrun it north?" he asked.

"No, it moves with the wind. That race we would lose. We must cross the Galana River."

"To the southwest, toward the fire?"

"It's our only chance. I've never seen one this big or moving this fast—"

Percival suddenly stopped speaking. He cocked his head, listening to the night. Then he grabbed both Hemingway and Mary by the arm and rushed them toward the only acacia tree near the camp. He shouted something in Maasai, and his porters dropped everything and ran after them.

"Up the tree, *now!*"

Just as they reached the tree, a stampede of animals of every type crashed into the camp.

The men shoved Mary up into the tree's great outstretched branches, then pulled themselves up into its open arms. One of the Maasai warriors slipped from the tree, and before he could get back up he was knocked to the ground by an antelope. His cries of pain were weakened with the impact of each hoof.

The animals, in their panicked escape, flooded by for what seemed like an eternity. Mary clung to the tree with all her might. Finally silence filled the air, mixed with smoke.

"Dammit," Percival said, "the fire is close. We need to run straight north and then turn west when we can, to get to the river."

"My notebooks!" Hemingway shouted.

"Papa, no!"

Hemingway slipped out of the tree and ran back toward the camp. It was smashed and already on fire. He rooted through the tattered remains of their tent, searching for the notebooks.

Percival caught up to him and tried to pull him away.

"No!" Hemingway said. "I won't lose any more work!"

He rummaged some more, finally grasping a satchel out of the flames. Percival pulled him clear and used his canteen to douse Hemingway's burning sleeves.

Both men looked up to see an old Maasai woman watching them. She pulled a tribal scarf over her head and disappeared into the smoke.

"Friend of yours, Papa?"

Hemingway could only stare in the direction she had gone.

* * *

They arrived at the river just ahead of the fire. Embers stung them as they slid down the bank into the cool waters.

Mary fought free of Hemingway. "No, Papa, we can't! The crocodiles!"

A crocodile splashed into the river. Its head exploded from a well-placed shot by Percival. More crocs slithered into the water, but now they were not interested in a fight; they swam straight for the fresh kill instead. Cannibalism was not beyond these ancient reptiles.

Hemingway pulled Mary past as they tore into the dead croc. Percival covered the crossing of the entire party. Only when all were across did he sling his rifle and wade in to cross himself.

One of the young crocs took an interest in him. He tried to unsling his rifle, but two shots rang out before he could. The croc went limp and floated away. Percival looked up to see Hemingway with a smoking .44 revolver in his hand.

On the far bank, Percival collapsed with the rest of the party, exhausted, in the mud.

An ember floated down near Hemingway's face, igniting a small bit of dry grass. He put it out with his muddy hand, then looked up to see a rain of embers drifting across the Galana.

He tapped Percival and pointed.

"Dammit," said Percival. "The wind has shifted with the dawn."

Hemingway nodded.

"Everyone up! We need to continue. The river will slow the fire, but soon this side will be ablaze."

"Where can we run to now?" Mary asked.

"We move laterally and pray the wind changes again."

* * *

Hours passed. When they could go no further without a rest, they took refuge from the sun below an acacia tree. Percival climbed it to check the progress of the fire. It was gaining on them. To the west, he saw a single dust trail.

"Papa, would you be so kind as to hand me the Springfield?"

Hemingway hefted up the Remington Springfield. Percival brought up the scope to see what was making the dust trail.

"Well, hello there."

A slow-moving Land Cruiser bumped along a rutted road.

Percival chambered a round, took careful aim, and shot out the right rear tire. Then he jumped down from the tree and handed Hemingway the rifle.

"All right, let's move. He might be quick on the change of that tire." Percival had a young Maasai tribesman run ahead, just to be sure.

They reached the vehicle just as its driver, Quentin Grogan, finished tightening the lug nuts.

"Did you have to shoot my tire, Philip?"

"I'm sorry, old boy, we were quite done in and couldn't give chase."

Red-hot embers were already falling around them. Quentin put the lug wrench away. "Well, shall we be off?"

"Yes, please," quipped Mary, who was putting salve on Hemingway's burnt arms.

They drove west. The overloaded vehicle was barely able to make twenty miles per hour. That speed just barely outpaced the fire as the afternoon wind picked up.

"Eventually we will run out of gas, gents," said Percival. "Then what?"

Quentin pointed ahead to Kilimanjaro. "Are you up for a little climb? A couple thousand feet should do; no need to summit."

Percival and Hemingway laughed. Mary did not.

They ran out of road at a thousand-foot elevation, and abandoned the Cruiser. They continued on by foot until they were a good twenty-five hundred feet above the brush line. There they set up camp with the limited supplies they had.

They sat in the setting sun and watched the fire line. It looked like a giant serpent writhing on the plain below. When it reached the foot of Kilimanjaro, it began to climb after them. An explosion announced it had reached the Land Cruiser.

"Well, there goes my Cruiser," said Quentin. "Pity. It was a good one."

"Look what I found!" shouted Hemingway. He held up a large flask. "Cocktail, anyone?"

* * *

That night the wind shifted, blowing southeast. Without fuel, the great Tsavo Wildfire of 1954 ended. By morning the sky had cleared, and nothing was left but the smell. A search aircraft circled them at noon, wagging its wings.

Percival smiled. "Quite an adventure, eh, Papa?"

"Best day of my life, Philip."

Hemingway had returned to Africa to rejuvenate, *esto vir*. He came as the hunter and ended up being hunted by the continent itself. That was acceptable. He was in the struggle, a part of it. And something else was present. He felt it. Knew it.

He was vulnerable—no longer the invincible apex predator. Now he was game, weakened by age and circumstance. A twinge of fear and a wave of depression settled over him, like the ash on the Tsavo Plain.

CHAPTER 38

TRUE AT FIRST LIGHT

1956

Hemingway and Mary traveled to Vienna after escaping Africa. There, he met with Adriana, hoping for inspiration. But he was different. She was different. This time her youth and beauty would not overcome his depression. He would not be inspired to write by her. His body was too broken. He was just clinging to his mind.

He won the Nobel Prize for Literature in October of 1954. Even this couldn't bring him out of his depressive state. His health was too shattered to allow him to travel to Stockholm to accept the honor. Instead, he asked the ambassador to read his speech. Before sending it, he read it aloud to Mary.

"Writing, at its best, is a lonely life. Organizations for writers palliate the writer's loneliness, but I doubt if they improve his writing. He grows in public stature as he sheds his loneliness, and often his work deteriorates. For he does his work alone, and if he is a good enough writer he must face eternity, or the lack of it, each day."

"That's pretty depressing, Papa. It reads like an obituary."

"And why do you think I have received the Nobel?"

Africa and a hard life had winded him. The headaches brought him to his knees. By the end of 1955 he was bedridden and forced to quit drinking. He began to heal, but he would never be the same.

Feeling better in early 1956, he tried to write again. But a skylight, boxing, car wrecks, and plane crashes all conspired to muddle his thoughts. A recurring nightmare jerked him awake; only sunlight drove her away.

He stepped out onto the veranda. Mary held out an iced tea from her chaise lounge. He shook it off and headed for the bar.

"How is your head?" she asked.

"Better." He poured a Bloody Mary. "I will try and work today."

"What are you working on?"

"Mary, you know I don't like to talk about work in progress."

"Yes, I know. Superstition and all. At least tell me the title."

The whine of a surplus US Army Jeep interrupted their conversation. Hemingway was quite familiar with the sound of its protestation as it climbed the hill. He had a Jeep too.

He walked to the driveway and watched as three heavily armed Cuban soldiers bounced in unison, lurching fore and aft as the four wheels alternately spun and dug in. Hemingway laughed in amusement.

"Don't antagonize them, Papa."

"They are just Batista thugs, Mary, more suited to fighting women and children."

"Still, we are in their country."

"They will not be in power much longer, I suspect."

A young arrogant captain stepped out of the Jeep as it ground to a halt. He was covered in orange dust and brushed at it as he approached.

"*Buenos dias*, Señor Hemingway."

Hemingway merely nodded in response.

"We have had reports of Communist rebels in this area, Señor. Have you seen anything suspicious?"

Hemingway shrugged his shoulders dismissively.

"There are rumors you support the Communists, as you did in Spain."

Finally Hemingway spoke. "There are many rumors on this little island, Captain. And while it is true I fought the Nazis and fascism in the thirties and forties, it is also true that I am too old now."

"There are many ways to support a movement, Señor."

"There are." Hemingway sipped his drink, never taking his eyes from the captain's.

"Indeed, Señor. Indeed." The captain turned to Mary. "Have a pleasant day, Señora."

"And you, Captain."

He remounted the vehicle with a false and ridiculous pomposity.

Ernest and Mary watched it until it rounded a corner at the bottom of the hill. Trees came to life as birds took flight with the echoing sounds of gunfire.

"Dammit!" Hemingway threw his crystal glass to the ground; it shattered on the rocks. Springing into action, he ran to his Jeep. As he got in he caught a glimpse of himself, white hair and beard. It surprised him for a fleeting moment.

Mary jumping into the passenger seat refocused him. He looked over at her, but didn't argue. He put the Jeep in gear and started down the hill.

They found the patrol at a sharp bend in the road, where they had to slow to a crawl. All three men were dead, their weapons gone. The captain stared at the sky with three eyes and a very surprised look on his face. A stream of blood wound its way down around his prominent nose.

"This will bring trouble to us, Papa."

"Shall we go visit Pio in Spain? He is not well."

Mary nodded in response, unable to take her eyes from the carnage.

*　*　*

Pio Baroja died shortly after Hemingway's arrival in Spain, and the experienced threatened to deepen Hemingway's despair. To ward it off, he sought respite in Paris.

He met with Picasso at the Ritz sidewalk café, the location of one of Hemingway's many victories. Picasso was still the most vibrant of his old friends; he seemed to never age. They talked of old times, laughed until they cried, and wept at the loss of the Lost Generation.

At a lull in conversation, a concierge stepped forward.

"Monsieur Hemingway, my manager has asked me to give you this suitcase. He believes it to be yours."

Hemingway took the bag and thanked the man. When the concierge had left, Hemingway clicked open the latches and looked inside.

"Well I'll be damned."

He heard a cackle from above, and his head snapped up. A black raven looked down on him from its perch on a lamppost.

Picasso was shuffling through the papers from the suitcase. "Is this...? Papa, how can it be?"

Hemingway let out a laugh and shook his head. "This is my work from the late twenties. I left these here in 1928. I completely forgot."

"Really, Papa, you must stop leaving your work lying about. Let's celebrate with champagne!"

Hemingway looked up at the raven once more. It stared back at him for a moment, then flew away cawing loudly.

CHAPTER 39

CHE TI DICE LA PATRIA?

The true nature of Communism showed itself in 1956 while they were in France. The Soviets crushed an uprising in Hungary with vengeance. After that, KGB Headquarters was a flurry of activity. Communiqués from field agents were piling up, as were transcripts of interviews of Hungarian activists and suspects. The mounting paperwork could not be processed quickly enough, and it was moved to basement storage, where it was stacked to a height of six feet. Hemingway's suitcase was there, too. Shoved to a corner and entombed by boxes of the damned.

When a tall sergeant did a quick inspection of the room, he noticed light emanating from the rear. Standing on his toes, he peered over the boxes. *Some idiot dropped a flashlight*, he thought. But he also felt a chill—an intense rush of unease, as if something evil was rushing toward him. Quickly he slammed the door shut, looped a brass date plate on a heavy padlock, and locked it. He shook the door to make sure it was sealed.

The suitcase had gained power. Each translation that lay within it, penned by an evil hand, had increased that power exponentially. Good and evil were in a constant struggle that resulted in equilibrium. One would not, could not, completely triumph over the other. They were locked in an endless ebb and flow, gain and loss.

Hemingway had gained. His recovery of his lost stories had given him what nothing else could: motivation. Not a rebirth, but a burst of energy when he needed it most.

He pulled himself from the threshold of death and returned to Cuba to write. By 1959, using his re-liberated stories, he had written *A Movable Feast, Islands in the Stream,* and over 20,000 words of what would become *True at First Light*. He even added chapters to the stalled *Garden of Eden*.

After locking the manuscripts, except *A Movable Feast,* in a safe deposit box in Havana, he entered a death spiral, from which he couldn't pull out.

Castro had seized power. Having flirted with Communism for most of his life, Hemingway joined the initial euphoria. But soon the beast rolled showing its underbelly: political prisoners, re-education camps, wanton executions. Even Hemingway's own profession came under attack. He added a new feeling: the self-loathing of guilt.

Cuban Communists were also seizing property and arresting anyone who dissented. It was as if Batista had returned, except there wasn't even the pretense of justice. Weak, disoriented, and paranoid, Hemingway decided to leave Cuba.

Havana's airport was bedlam. Panic had set in when Castro's thugs swept into the airport, pulled people out of line, and dragged them off. Flashing their passports from the United States, Ernest and Mary managed to make it through to a makeshift customs office.

Hemingway's hands shook as he turned at the top of the air stairs for a last glimpse of his home. He saw her there, taunting him, laughing at him.

Turning, he shuffled with the gait of an old man into the Pan Am DC-4.

"After all, it really is Martha's," he mumbled as they passed through the door.

CHAPTER 40

THE END OF SOMETHING

1960

Hemingway traveled alone to Spain for a photo session with *Life* magazine. He had struggled through the story, and it ended up being much longer than they wanted. His mind was hesitant, unsure. He had returned to a familiar subject, bullfighting, hoping it would help him. And it did... to a point. In September of 1960, the first of three segments were published, to good reviews.

He was still in Spain when the press announced his demise for a third time. He wired Mary that he was fine, but in fact he was quite sick and near a breakdown. He returned to New York.

There, his paranoia returned. He shut himself up in Mary's apartment and refused to leave. Darting from window to window, he peeked out looking for the FBI.

"Papa, please sit down."

"They are out there, Mary. Now that Cuba is with the Soviets, Hoover will come for me."

"Ernest, that is ridiculous."

"And that damn Gypsy! She has my manuscripts in Havana. I'll never get them now."

"Papa, stop it. They are in a safe deposit box…"

"She knows. She knows where my suitcase is, too!"

Mary packed up that night and took Hemingway to Idaho. She didn't want the press, or anyone else, to see him like this.

* * *

Back in nature, Hemingway became a seesaw of emotion. After yet another car accident, in which he broke his arm, he was unable to write at all. Without its distraction, he spun out of control.

In November, he was checked into the Mayo Clinic in Minnesota. He thought it was for hypertension. Instead, he was dosed with electricity. It ripped through his brain, attacking synapses, memory, mind. As he writhed on the table, strapped to it as if he were being tortured, he fought to hold on to even a single thought.

He turned his head to the side trying to ease the searing pain. The tight white braid of the nurse was clear even through the chaos of his electrified mind.

No. It can't be.

Thrashing at the restraints, he fought to get free.

A voice with a slight Hungarian accent tried to calm him. It only sent him into greater frenzy.

"Maximum power. Quickly."

Voltage struck him like a bolt of lightning. He heard a clap of thunder and stared at the nurse with horror until he passed out.

"That was quite an adverse reaction, Doctor," said the young blonde nurse.

"Yes, it was. Most unusual."

* * *

Barbaric electroshock therapy had done what war, accidents, alcohol, and time couldn't. It had robbed Hemingway of his thoughts, his mind, his essence. He was unable to form coherent thought, let alone write.

And even here, in the valley of the sun, he could not hold back the darkness. It fell upon him with ever-increasing weight. Mary wouldn't leave him. Even when she went to the store, she insisted on taking him with her.

On one such trip, he fell asleep, so she left him in the car while she went inside. He was awoken by a horn blast—a pickup truck honking at an old Indian woman in a red bandana. Hemingway put on his glasses to see clearly. *The Gypsy*. Was it real? Or his electrocuted mind?

Her words came to him. *It is your curse too, even if by half.*

He stumbled out of the car and across the street, dodging a bus. But she was gone. On the ground where she had stood was a small flower. It shriveled in the afternoon sun.

His refuge in nature was no longer a sanctuary. No longer could he open his eyes and see the light of its beauty. Even here, he was stalked.

When Mary caught him with a gun in his lap, he was returned to the Mayo Clinic for more erasing. But it didn't matter. He was gone. Not just his memory, but his soul. It had fallen into an endless abyss while he was strapped to that table.

She had finally won.

All that was left was the corpse of the undead.

He knew how to take care of it. He got his favorite gun, a double-barreled shotgun, out of the cabinet. Papa wanted one more glimpse.

He shuffled to the front door and opened it. His weak eyes squinted at the July morning sun. Blinded by the white light, he closed them and breathed it in instead.

He placed the wilted flower in his mouth and took one last glance at life. His fear was gone. His mind resolute.

I would have liked to have read my suitcase's contents.

Poor Hadley.

CHAPTER 41

IN OUR TIME

1992

The heavy padlock fell to the concrete floor, and the CIA agent handed the bolt cutter to an old bent-over sergeant. The sergeant looked over the agent's shoulder trying to see through the small window. Picking up the brass tag, Agent Cranz flipped it in his hand and read the Cyrillic: *Hungarian Revolt, 1956.*

Feeling crowded, Professor Cranz turned to the sergeant. "Need something?"

The man shook his head and pulled on the door handle. It opened with a gush of air and a moan of the hinges, as if an ancient tomb had been violated. Squinting into the room, the sergeant jumped when Cranz asked him what he saw.

"Nothing."

He motioned his men to begin emptying the room, then left.

These old Soviets sure are weird, Cranz thought.

His mastery of Russian was perfect. He had been an associate professor of Russian Literature at Princeton before volunteering for the CIA.

It seemed his penchant for young co-eds had drawn attention. It had been so simple at first: a position of power, a young impressionable woman. But he had gotten impatient, had grown tired of the game. Turning to chemistry to aid his debauchery. One strong-willed co-ed had taken exception to this and confronted him. He had to make her disappear. And while she would never be found, he thought it best that he, too, disappear. For a while.

After this experience in Russia, he could return to a full professorship. And with what the CIA had taught him, his former passions would be more safely pursued.

After the collapse of the Soviet Union, Russia and all its former states were plunged into chaos. CIA agents were everywhere, and he was literally reading the KGB's mail. As a bonus, Moscow was full of young, desperate women.

Cranz had the men spread the boxes all down the long hallway. His task was to look for intel on CIA agents that had disappeared during the Hungarian Revolt. Not that it mattered to him. They were long dead. How was inconsequential.

For thirty years, it had lay dormant in its sarcophagus, and now it sat in the weak flickering light of bad fluorescents. An alligator skin suitcase. It stood out among all the boxes.

"What is this one?" he asked aloud.

A corporal who had set it down just shrugged and walked off, leaving him in the hall alone.

Cranz read the tag: *Trial of Colonel Petrovski/Subversive Literature*.

He heard a noise behind him, and looked over his shoulder. "Anyone there?"

There was no response.

A rat scurried out of the room, making him jump. When he regained his composure, he shook a Marlboro cigarette out of the pack and lit it. He took a long drag.

"I wouldn't do that here," said a voice.

"Jesus!" He jumped again.

An old cleaning woman in a babushka approached. She grimaced through stained, craggy teeth.

"He is not here," she said. "And neither should that cigarette be. You will start a fire."

"Everything here is damp and moldy. It will not burn. And who would care, old woman? Go away."

She pushed her wheeled bucket down the hall. Her long white braid swayed as she walked.

Cranz turned his attention back to the suitcase. He wiped the dust off the locks and clicked them. He thought he heard the old woman cackle.

He pulled out a sheaf of papers. Strange—though old, these were not damp. And they appeared to be… a novel? In Russian. He rifled through some more papers. These were written in German. *What the hell?*

He returned the papers to the suitcase and snapped it shut.

*   *   *

Making his way to the sergeant's office he entered. He began to speak, but the attention of the sergeant was on the suitcase.

"I'll take care of this myself sergeant. Same deal as before. Tell your men 100$ for each file that mentions CIA. Don't try and bull shit me, I will know any without mold are fakes."

At the Hilton Moscow Leningradskaya Hotel, Cranz studied the manuscripts. His German was not that good, but he could see that it was definitely a translation of the Russian work. He began to sort the sheaves of paper into stacks. Some were stories, others were longer works. And still there were more manuscripts in the case.

"I'm bored."

The prostitute he'd ordered upon his return to the hotel still lay naked across the pillows. He raised her chin, caressing it, then slapped her hard.

"Get off the bed."

She fled to the bathroom as he returned to the suitcase.

"It can't be."

These manuscripts were in English. He paged through them, then stacked each on top of its Russian and German translations.

He knew exactly what he had.

This is Hemingway's lost suitcase. They were stealing his work.

She came out of the bathroom fully clothed. He grabbed her around the waist to stop her.

"I'm sorry, baby," he said.

"You are mean, like Russian."

"Then you should be used to it."

CHAPTER 42

A WAY YOU'LL NEVER BE

Envy raged into a state of psychosis, always searching, never finding words, neither his nor Hemingway's. He had spent over fifty years confined to the Bohnice Psychiatric Hospital in Prague. There he passed his time trying to write, and his frustration at failures only reinforced the impression that he was unstable.

In 1939, he had been caught in the Nazi invasion of Czechoslovakia while trying to get back to Paris. After his interview by the Gestapo, he was declared insane. His only concern had been a suitcase full of stories. His foreign passport prevented the Nazis from sending him to a death camp, so they turned him over to the Czech authorities, who put him in Bohnice.

Nothing changed when the Soviets took over. But now that the Soviet Union had collapsed—he was free. At the age of ninety-two.

He was in surprisingly good health, and there was no reason not to let him return to Paris.

He took his seat on the Aeroflot Yakovlev 42, which was delayed as they waited for connecting passengers from Moscow. When at last they boarded, a young man came down the aisle and opened the overhead bin across from his seat, setting his baggage down as he did.

The old man stared at the bag, his eyes wide. He ran his hand across the old alligator skin.

"Where did you get this bag, young man?" he asked in French.

But Cranz didn't understand French. He jerked the bag away and stuffed it in the overhead.

*   *   *

Mid-flight, after a couple of beers, Cranz went to the lavatory. The old man seized his opportunity. He stood from his seat and opened the suitcase without removing it from the overhead bin. It wouldn't open all the way in the tight space, but he could see the manuscripts. He knew.

Cranz appeared at his side. He slammed the bag shut and glared at the old man. They both knew.

The seat belt sign came on; they were descending into Paris. A flight attendant directed them to their seats. Even as they sat, their eyes stayed locked across the aisle.

Turning final the captain called for full flaps. As they were extending, a jackscrew on the left wing failed. Its flaps retracted due to the wind force as the right wing's flaps extended. Asymmetric lift rolled the Yak-42. The crew fought for control. They got the aircraft upright, but it was too late—they were too low to recover. Trees' outstretched limbs pulled the craft from the air.

It impacted two miles short of Charles de Gaulle Airport and broke apart.

A layer of cloud rose, looking more like a mist. Slowly it consumed the half moon, giving it an hourglass shape as its light fought to be free.

*   *   *

He stood unmoved by the carnage that lay on the earth. A cold and petty man of failure. He had aspired to be a writer, but had no compassion and a soul that was impure. He could not write credibly of the human condition, because he didn't feel it. He was a parasite, submitting cold, lifeless reports to a third-rate paper. Usually in the travel section, simply describing hotels. He wasn't assigned this story; he had happened upon it.

Glancing to his left, the dead eyes of an old man returned his stare. The body was shattered and twisted. *Strange*, he thought. Not at all like the movies, where they merely looked asleep. *I can use that in my story.*

A charred suitcase lay slightly open at his feet. Emergency lights strobed its contents. His gaze landed on a title—a manuscript. A blue carbon blew against his leg, and he bent down to grab it.

His eyes went wide when he saw Hemingway's name. Then the date. He had read all of Hemingway's work. This was unpublished. Could this be the famed lost suitcase from Paris? The dates were right.

He knelt in front of the suitcase, his hands trembling. He coveted a skill like Hemingway's, but knew he could never possess it. Even now, as he stood in the middle of a human tragedy, he knew all he could manage would be a sterile accounting.

His eyes darted around the scene, looking to see if he had been noticed. The moon had settled below the haze, losing its shape in the layers of cloud. It had darkened to a red hue. Firemen were busy putting out the fire on the tail section. No one looked his way.

He closed the suitcase and slipped away into the darkness.

An ancient woman watched as he disappeared. She pulled up her scarf and faced the fire, which danced across her craggy features. Her sharp teeth grew into a smile, and she cackled at the night.

THE END

Leland Shanle has also written the award winning Aviator Series: Project 7 Alpha, Vengeance at Midway and Guadalcanal, Endgame in the Pacific and Code Name: Infamy.

http://www.lelandshanle.com

https://www.amazon.com/Leland-Shanle/e/B002BLUC72/
ref=dp_byline_cont_ebooks_1

www.ingramcontent.com/pod-product-compliance
Lightning Source LLC
Chambersburg PA
CBHW030501260626
47157CB00005B/1596